Loving Brooke

Elsa Winckler

Loving Brooke
Copyright © 2022 Elsa Winckler
All rights reserved.

ISBN: (print) 978-1-958136-10-2

Inkspell Publishing
207 Moonglow Circle #101
Murrells Inlet, SC 29576

Edited By Rie Langdon
Cover Art By Fantasia Frog

DEDICATION

To Mia, our beautiful daughter who has been brave enough to give love a second chance.

ELSA WINCKLER

CHAPTER 1

A kiss? *Seriously.*

Baffled, Brooke put the paintbrush down, her gaze never leaving the painting she'd just finished. She was known for her "vividly realized oil landscape paintings," as an art journal had once hailed one of her pieces. And recently, another critic had raved about her work, describing one of her paintings as "simple, bold forms expressed in strong strokes and richly saturated colors."

Okay, lately, she'd moved away from only doing landscape painting and had begun to explore the human figure, but what she'd done on this canvas was something entirely different.

This was a kiss. No matter how or from which angle she looked at the finished work in front of her, there was no doubt about the subject matter.

The faces of the couple kissing were shadowy, their features indistinct, but they were kissing—that much was clear. Ardently kissing, to be precise. But gone were the "bold strokes and richly saturated colors." Instead, muted hues created a dreamlike glow inside of which scratchy brushstrokes swirled around to form lips, kissing.

And why did the blurry features look so familiar?

With unsteady fingers, Brooke tried to comb back her hair. She hadn't been sleeping well; that was probably the reason she was seeing things that weren't there.

Irritated, she brushed another piece of hair out of her face. Why was her hair all over the place? Hadn't she put it up in a ponytail that morning? Patting her head, she tried to find the scrunchie she'd used for the ponytail earlier. Where was it? Shaking her head, she dropped her hand. She couldn't even remember, as she'd been so wrapped up in getting these images onto a canvas, in capturing the restlessness she'd been experiencing over the last few weeks. What she hadn't expected, though, was that the end result would be…a kiss.

Grabbing a cloth to try to clean the worst of the paint on her hands, she checked the clock on the wall. Connor should be home soon.

She seriously didn't have time for this. It was the second week in June, and there were still several paintings she had to finish for an exhibition in Seattle in the middle of July. The gallery in Livingston, the one that would be showcasing her work moving forward, also wanted more than the two paintings she was in the process of forwarding from a gallery in Missoula to them. On top of that, she and Connor would be moving to the ranch in two weeks' time.

Schools were also about to close for the summer holidays, and when Connor was home, she didn't get anything done during the day. She loved having her son around, but at nearly seven, her little boy had boundless energy and he kept her busy. Any work she was thinking of doing during summer break, she'd have to do once he went to sleep at night.

Determined, Brooke picked up the brush again. Okay, she hadn't been kissed in a while. Quite a while, actually. That was probably the reason why her subconscious had conjured up this scene.

Fortunately, she had no qualms about changing a

painting if she didn't like the end result, and she definitely didn't like this one. With a few strokes of her brush, she'd be able to transform it in seconds.

Purposefully, she moved toward the painting, but before she could bring the brush down, the door behind her flew open.

"I thought you must be painting; you didn't even hear me knock! I've just been to my Pilates class and thought I'd better check and see whether there is still food in the house."

It was her mother. Brooke swallowed a groan. Her mom had a knack for turning up at the least opportune moments and this was definitely one of those. The last thing she wanted to do was to try to explain what she'd just painted.

Moving so her body would, hopefully, shield the painting from her mom's eyes, Brooke smiled. "Mom! So nice to see you. Come on, I'll make tea—"

But her mother never missed a thing. Unceremoniously, she shoved Brooke out of the way. "I was wondering what's keeping you so busy!" Clasping her hands together, she inhaled sharply. "Brooke...oh, my dear girl, this is so, so beautiful. Different from anything you've done before, but so powerful. Look at the emotion, the feeling, the heat. No wonder I've been struggling to get hold of you for days."

"I don't like it. I'm going to paint over it—"

Her mother turned on her, eyes blazing. "You'll do no such thing! This is one of the best paintings you've ever done, and deep down, you know it. You simply must make this one part of your upcoming exhibition in Seattle. If you don't want to do that, at least give it to the gallery in Missoula; they'll be thrilled to add this to your collection. I'll go with you—"

"Don't be ridiculous, Mom. I paint landscapes—"

"Yes, but you've been painting human figures, as well—"

3

"Those works are something entirely different." Shaken, Brooke motioned toward the painting. "I have no idea where this one comes from, but it's not something I'll send to any gallery."

"Of course, you will. Mark my words, people are going to be talking about this work for a long time." She glanced back at it over her shoulder. "As for the subject matter—I don't think it's so strange for you to be thinking about kissing someone—"

"I'm not thinking of kissing anyone! Seriously, Mother!" Brooke exclaimed, more heatedly than she'd intended.

Her mother carried on as if she hadn't spoken at all. "You've been alone since Adam's passing three years ago, my dear. He was sweet, a wonderful husband to you and a great father to Connor, but it's high time for you to think about kissing someone again." Her eyes twinkled. "You're right, your subconscious is definitely trying to tell you something. Maybe kissing someone like—"

"Don't even say it, please, Mom, really—"

"—the very sexy Gavin Wilson." Again, she glanced back at the painting. "I have to say, the one shadowy figure does look an awful lot like Gavin, don't you think? And the woman?" She looked at Brooke. "She could be you."

Brooke quickly glanced at her work and nearly groaned out loud. Her mother was right. She saw what Brooke hadn't wanted to acknowledge—she'd painted Gavin Wilson kissing...well, her.

Agitated, she turned away. "Of course, I haven't painted him. Seriously, Mom, I don't know how many times I must tell you—Gavin and I are friends. This is becoming so boring. You and I have been friends with his sisters since they arrived in Alisson from South Africa nearly three years ago. Since Gavin has moved in with Charlie and Lindsay, he's become a friend; it's not that strange. We're friends. We talk sometimes when the family gets together, but that's only when you or Charlie or

4

Lindsay invite Connor and me for dinner. Otherwise, I never see him."

"You could always invite him over, you know. I hate to see you so alone."

"Mom, please stop. I'm not alone, I have Connor. And just for the record, I'm very happy on my own, doing my own thing. When Adam was alive, he let me paint while he took care of the rest, and I happily went along with it. Only after he was gone, I realized how little I knew about our finances. It took me a long time to figure out what was going on. With Logan's help and your attorney's assistance, I'm finally at a place where I feel I'm in control of my own life. I'm not about to ever let another man 'fix' everything for me."

"Oh, sweetie, Adam spoiled you because he loved you. And you never questioned his decisions. He left you and Connor well provided for, remember? You can't let the past hold you back. Keep moving forward. And, oh, you and Gavin will make such a lovely couple, and think of the beautiful babies—"

"Mom!" Brooke called out, and grabbing her mother's arm, she steered her down the stairs toward the kitchen. "Come on, I'll make tea and you—"

"—the two of you will make." Her mom was on a roll. "You with your beautiful blond hair and Gavin with his gorgeous blue eyes…"

They stepped into the kitchen. Time for a different tactic. "Tell me about little Ellie. Have you managed to finish unpacking in between playing with baby?"

Fortunately, talking about her new granddaughter and her recent move to Logan's ranch was something guaranteed to get her mom to change topics immediately. Her brother Logan's and his wife Charlie's baby had been born in March, and they all immediately fell in love with the tiny girl. Brooke's mother was completely besotted.

She put the kettle on. Thank goodness her mom had stopped talking about Gavin. It was so annoying having to explain over and over that they were just friends.

"Such a fabulous idea Logan had—all of us living on the ranch—I couldn't be happier. Yesterday, I babysat Ellie when Charlie and Logan had to go to Bozeman. When she cries, I take her for a stroll. Oh, Brooke, I love it there, and I can't wait for you to join us in a week's time."

Brooke groaned. "Don't remind me. I have the upcoming exhibition in Seattle in the middle of July. I'm moving the two paintings still in the gallery in Missoula to a lovely one in Livingston that also wants more paintings, and—"

"Why? You've been with that gallery for such a long time?"

"I think I told you. Lynda, the owner, is on a cruise, touring the Mediterranean, and she's decided to appoint a manager. The last time we spoke, she said she'd still be working with the artists, but the new manager will run the day-to-day sales."

"So what's the problem? Don't you and the new manager get along?" her mom asked.

"I don't…like the vibe any longer. Besides, Livingstone is much closer." Her mom didn't have to know about the manager's not-so-subtle creepy advances. Fortunately, she was in the position where galleries were asking her if they could exhibit her work, not the other way round. The gallery in Livingston was in the process of organizing a fine art firm to fetch the two paintings—on Wednesday—that were still hanging in the gallery in Missoula. When that was done, she'd have one less worry.

"Anyway, schools are closing in two weeks, and with Connor around…"

"Well, fortunately, I don't have an immediate upcoming exhibition. There is one in November in Butte, but I have more than enough time to be ready by then. Please, let him stay with me on the ranch, even if it's only for a few days. Everyone will spoil him rotten; you won't have to worry about him and can finish your paintings."

"Thanks, Mom, but—"

"He'll so enjoy the wide-open spaces on the ranch, and you know how much he loves the animals." As usual, her mom wasn't listening. "He gets on so well with Gavin, doesn't he?"

Brooke laughed. "Mom, you're relentless. Give it a rest, will you? Your son is married to the love of his life, thanks to your meddling."

"I didn't meddle. I simply made sure they got together in one room. The rest happened without any help from me."

"That's meddling, Mom. You deliberately let him believe Charlie was a man!"

"I never said that. Anyway, they were meant to be together—anyone can see that. When Charlie and Lindsay moved to Alisson about two… no, it's nearly three years now, I just knew she and Logan were meant to be together. The same with Lindsay and Blake. I vividly remember the night Blake joined us at the bar. His gaze zeroed in on Lindsay, and he couldn't look away. It was so obvious then they belonged together. That's why I know you and—"

"Mom, stop it!" Brooke groaned. "Can we please talk about something else? How is Lindsay?"

Her mother smiled. "She's absolutely glowing. Being pregnant seems to agree with the Wilson sisters. She's been very busy; their website for her lovely products seems to be a hit, and they can't keep up with the orders. Apparently, Lilly will take over the running of the place when Baby comes, and Lindsay will probably have to get another person in to help during those first few weeks."

Brooke smiled. "How wonderful she's also expecting a little girl."

Her mother's eyes twinkled. "But now we need to find a little brother for Connor."

"Mom! I'm thirty-three and I have a child—not an attractive package deal for any man, even if I was looking for one. Which I'm not."

"Oh, sweetie, that's ridiculous, you're gorgeous, and the right man—"

"Not interested, Mom. I have Connor. I'm very happy."

Her mom glanced at her watch. "Where is he, by the way? Shouldn't he be back from school?"

Brooke looked at the clock against the wall and frowned. Her mom was right. Connor should've been home by now. Her house was close to the school and he was usually here about ten minutes after the school day ended.

Before she could react, there was a knock on the door.

"You expecting anyone?" her mom asked.

Brooke shook her head while she walked toward the front door and opened it. She blinked, but she wasn't hallucinating. On her porch, with Connor next to him, was Gavin Wilson holding two bags of what looked like groceries in his hands, if she wasn't mistaken.

Speechless, she could only stare. Fortunately, Connor started babbling the minute she opened the door. "I told him we can just open the door, but he wanted to knock." Connor hugged her legs. "Hi, Mom, I'm hungry. I've fetched Uncle Gavin to cook for us. Where is Grandma? I saw her car. Grandma!" he yelled and rushed inside.

Stunned, Brooke stared after Connor.

Gavin cleared his throat. "I found him at my front door."

"What do you mean?"

"Connor. He came to the house."

"I don't believe it. But...why?"

Gavin grinned. "He's told you." He lifted the two bags of groceries he was carrying. "I'm happy to oblige."

Brooke frowned. Had she heard correctly? Her son had gone to Gavin's house to ask him to come and cook for them?

"But...it's totally ridiculous; you can't come and cook

for us. Gavin, really…"

"It's no secret in town you and your mother…how shall I put it? You don't like cooking?"

"I cook," Brooke began heatedly, but before she could finish her sentence, her mother appeared, all smiles.

"Yes, my dear girl, we cook, but nobody wants to eat what we cook! Come on in, Gavin, I'm on my way. I'm so glad you're here."

Gavin smiled. "Hi, Eleanor, lovely to see you."

Beaming, her mom gave Brooke a quick hug. "I still have some things to do before I drive back to the ranch. Enjoy your dinner!" She stopped halfway down the stairs to look back at them. "Gavin, ask Brooke to show you her new painting."

Brooke gnashed her teeth. "Goodbye, Mother." She quickly closed the door before her mom could utter something even more embarrassing.

"I'm so sorry Connor bothered you. I'll talk to him. You really don't have to cook for us."

"What about bourbon-grilled pork chops?"

Her tummy growled.

Gavin grinned. "I'll take that as a yes."

For some reason, he was never quite prepared for her. Gavin busied himself getting the groceries he'd bought out of the bag. Ever since he'd arrived to visit his sisters in Alisson during the middle of last year, Brooke Johnson had caught his eye.

Initially, he'd thought it was because of the sadness he'd noticed in her startling blue eyes, but the longer time he'd spent in the presence of the honey-blond widow, the more she kinda…what? Bothered him? Maybe. There was something in the air when he was around her. She was gorgeous, sexy and…off limits. He was very much aware of that fact.

Which, of course, begged the question: why was he

here, in her kitchen, about to cook for her and her son?

Brooke was crouching in front of Connor. "What are you supposed to do after school?"

"Come back home. But, Mo-o-m..."

"Correct. You come home. I didn't know where you were. I was worried."

"I'm sorry," Connor mumbled before he flashed his mother a smile. "But aren't you glad we're not having sandwiches again?"

Brooke quickly got up. "That's enough, Connor. Do you know how many kids don't have any food?"

"Yeah, I know. But—"

"But nothing. You'll apologize to Uncle Gavin for bothering him."

"But Grandma said Uncle Gavin is a marvelous cook," Connor said. "So I thought it would be nice to have someone who is a marvelous cook, cook for us. And you're working so hard—aren't you glad?"

Brooke's mouth twitched. Connor had perfectly mimicked his grandma's "marvelous."

Gavin had to swallow his own grin. "It's really no bother. I have to eat anyway." He gave Connor a wink.

Connor grinned. "See? He's not bothered. Can I go and play until we eat, Mom?"

"May I," Brooke corrected him.

"May I?" He grinned cheekily.

"Yes, go play, but you and I are going to have another conversation about this."

"But only after we've eaten, please?"

Brooke burst out laughing and hugged her son. "Yes, sweetie, we'll eat first."

Gavin turned away. Brooke laughed easily and often. It was one of the first things he'd noticed about her. One of her smiles always seemed to light up a room. And her gorgeous legs had led to a number of near-embarrassing moments for him.

Connor left, and after a few minutes, Gavin saw

Brooke fidgeting. It was clear she was very uncomfortable having him in her kitchen. Interesting. Normally, she seemed unfazed. He'd been to her house before, although this was the first time neither of his sisters was with him. Could that be the reason why?

He set the oven to broil and took out the meat. "A small saucepan?" he asked.

Wordlessly, she handed him one.

"This looks brand new," he said, putting it over an open flame.

"Not quite," she said. "I don't...okay, I don't cook. I can't cook. I don't think I've ever used that. Happy?"

Grinning, he opened the bottle of bourbon he'd bought, poured a quarter of a cup into the saucepan, added brown sugar, mustard, and garlic. While he waited for the ingredients to boil, he looked at Brooke. "This isn't a competition."

She'd moved closer and was watching his every move. "Tell me what you're doing. It smells divine."

"It's a very easy recipe. You stir these ingredients until it boils..." He kept stirring for a while. "There it is—then you turn down the heat and let it simmer for a while until it thickens slightly."

"Where did you learn to cook?"

"When our parents died, Charlie and Lindsay were in their early twenties and still studying. I tried to make things easy for them when they came home over weekends and holidays. I didn't realize how much I'd picked up from our mom—she was a great cook. Once I started, I discovered I love to cook."

Brooke grinned. "Well, that explains it. My mom, as everyone knows, is a terrible cook. In our house, my dad was the one who made sure we had something to eat, but after he passed away, we were basically raised on sandwiches. I make a mean sandwich if you ever want one."

"I'll remember that." He smiled. "Your mom has other

strengths, though. She's a great artist, like you are. We all have our strengths and weaknesses." He motioned toward the oven. "It's going to take a few minutes to grill the chops. Why don't you show me your new painting?"

"No!" she called out before she turned away quickly. "What about wine? I have a bottle of Chardonnay…"

"I've also brought a bottle of wine, but yeah, thanks, a glass of Chardonnay sounds lovely. Why don't you want me to see your p—?"

"So have you decided if you're moving to the ranch?" Brooke interrupted while she poured the wine.

"Yes, now that I've joined Logan's firm, it will make things easier. We've talked about building offices adjacent to the main homestead on the ranch for the times—" His phone rang before he could finish his sentence. "Sorry, it's Charlie."

He answered while he took his glass from Brooke. Their fingers touched briefly. She caught her breath, turned away quickly. Mmmm, interesting evening all around.

"Charlie? Everything okay?" he asked his sister.

"Yes, of course. I was just checking up on you. I haven't heard from you this week."

"I had lunch with you on the ranch on Saturday; it's Monday."

"Really? Well, I've missed you. What are you doing?"

And then the penny dropped. "Ah. Now I get it. You've spoken to Eleanor?"

At the mention of her mother's name, Brooke whipped around, her eyes wide.

"No, I phoned her to remind her to buy diapers for Elly…"

"And let me guess, then she just happened to mention that I was cooking for Brooke and Connor?"

"Oh, I can't tell you how happy I am to hear that!" Charlie gushed. "We've all been hoping the two of you—"

But Brooke grabbed his phone before Charlie could

finish her sentence.

"Charlie, you know what my mom is like. Please ignore her. Gavin and I are friends. Nothing else. Friends. I wish you'd stop this."

Gavin popped the chops in the oven, his eyes never leaving Brooke's face. It was fascinating watching all the emotions on her face and…was she blushing? Brooke quickly turned her back on him, but he'd already seen her slightly rosy cheeks.

While talking, Brooke bent down to pick up one of Connor's trucks on the floor. Her jeans slid down slightly, and for a millisecond, a tiny piece of white lace was visible.

Desire slammed into his gut, and the blood roared in his ears. What the hell had just happened?

CHAPTER 2

Out of breath, Brooke turned back with Gavin's phone still clutched tightly in her hands. "I'm sorry about my mother. She is incorrigible, and I have no excuses to offer for her. For some or other reason, she's decided she's a matchmaker. You'll remember how she conned Logan to go and see Charlie. I've tried to explain to both your sisters, time and time again, that you and I are just friends, but now that they are happily married, they seem to be helping my mother with her matchmaking plans—as if she needs any encouragement. When you see them again, please make sure they understand we're friends, and that's it?"

Gavin opened his mouth, but Connor came rushing in, cutting off his words.

"I'm hungry, Mom. Really, really hungry."

"I'm going to make some fries, as well. Do you think you can wait a little while longer?" Gavin asked Connor while peeling the potatoes he'd brought with him.

"Can I watch what you're doing?" Connor asked, eyes wide.

"Of course. Pull up a chair—you can help me."

Within seconds, Connor was standing on a chair and

with his hand on Gavin's shoulder.

Brooke swallowed against the lump in her throat. Connor obviously had the need of a male figure in his life. He loved hanging out with her brother, Logan, and since the first night they'd met Gavin, her little boy had somehow made a connection with the tall, seriously gorgeous guy.

Yeah, she'd noticed exactly how gorgeous he was. She was a widow, not dead. And one would have to be dead not to notice Gavin Wilson's cobalt blue eyes or the movement of his arm muscles beneath a shirt or the way his jeans fitted over...

Taking a big sip from her wine, she turned away. Oh, my goodness, look at the direction her thoughts were going. *Focus, focus.* There had to be something else that she should be doing besides drooling over Gavin. Oh, yes, the table. She could set the table—that at least she could do. Quickly, she walked toward the cupboard where she kept the silverware and plates.

Her body was buzzing, though, making it difficult to focus. What was it that she'd thought of doing? She stared at the cupboard in front of her for a few minutes before she remembered. Set the table. Take out knives, forks, plates, napkins.

Help.

Inhaling deeply, she tried to concentrate on the task at hand, but it was difficult. Before Connor had reappeared in the kitchen, she and Gavin had been alone in a room for the first time ever. A room still vibrating with electricity.

By the time they'd finished dinner, the unfamiliar undercurrents in the kitchen had Gavin seriously hot and bothered. What the hell was going on? For some strange reason, his whole being had tuned into Brooke, and all his senses were on high alert—without looking at her, he was conscious of her every move, her smell, the light on her hair, her full mouth.

This had never happened before. He liked the opposite sex—he'd dated often—but what was going on in this kitchen tonight was a first.

Fortunately, Connor had kept the conversation flowing since neither he nor Brooke seemed to have much to say. He'd made the food, and he knew it was a foolproof recipe, but he might as well been eating dust. He'd hardly tasted anything.

Brooke finally got up. "Time for bed, Connor. Go take a bath. I'll be up in a minute."

Reluctantly, Connor got up. "Uncle Gavin, you'll read me a story when I'm in bed?"

Brooke didn't look at Gavin but shook her head. "Sweetheart, Uncle Gavin wants to go home…"

"Of course, I will," Gavin heard himself say. "While you have your bath, I'll clean up here, and then I can read you a story."

Brooke shook her head. "That's not necessary, Gavin, really. You've cooked; I'll wash. I just want to…"

They simultaneously reached to pick up the same plate, and again their fingers brushed briefly. Brooke snatched her hand away quickly, but not before he noticed the soft blush on her cheeks.

"Come on, Connor, let me help you." Without looking back, Brooke took Connor by the hand, and they left the kitchen.

Gavin exhaled slowly. He wasn't sure what was going on here tonight, but he had to get out of her house before he did something really stupid. Like touching Brooke's face to find out if her skin was actually as soft as it looked. Or, heaven forbid, kissing her. He kept looking at her soft lips, and okay, yeah, it wasn't the first time he'd noticed just how inviting her lips were, but tonight she had him twisted up in knots. The fact that she was totally unaware of the effect she had on him made it worse.

Cussing softly, he cleared the table. He had no business

lusting after Brooke. Relationships were complicated, he'd learned after the brief time he'd spent with Sarah, his last attempt at dating, and when he'd found out she'd been sleeping with someone else the whole time they were together, he'd been more relieved than anything else. *You are not relationship material,* she'd told him. Why she hadn't conveyed that fact and broken it off with him, before she'd jumped into bed with someone else, would remain a mystery.

He was all too aware of the fact he was nobody's hero. He'd even failed to notice that one of his own sisters was having problems with the guy she'd been dating. Only when his sisters informed him they were moving to Alisson, in Montana, halfway around the globe, had he learned about the harrowing time Lindsay had dealing with Mark Taylor, her boyfriend at the time. And then he also hadn't been here when Lindsay needed his help when the same Taylor followed her and put both her and Charlie's lives in danger.

If it hadn't been for Blake Davidson, the ex-FBI agent who was now his brother-in-law, Lindsay would probably have been hurt again, or worse.

He could cook for Brooke and her son, but even thinking of getting closer to the two of them would be a huge mistake.

"Gavin?"

Brooke was behind him, but he finished cleaning the cupboard before he turned to face her. "Connor in bed?"

"Yes, I'm sorry, but he keeps asking for you. I tried…"

"It's not a problem. I loved listening to stories, too, when I was his age."

"Up the stairs, first door to the left. Coffee?"

"Thanks, yes." He slipped out without him meeting her eyes. What the hell? He should've said he had to go, not agreed to stay even longer in the company of the lovely widow.

When Brooke peeped into Connor's room a little later, her son was fast asleep, but there was no sign of Gavin. Frowning, she tucked the blankets around her little boy and kissed him on the forehead before she tiptoed out. It hadn't taken her that long to switch on the coffee machine and to take out mugs. She'd thought Gavin would still be reading to Connor. So where was he?

It was around nine o'clock, and although the sun had already disappeared behind the mountains, it wasn't yet dark outside.

As she closed Connor's door behind her, she noticed the light in the room she used for her studio. The painting. Oh, no, Gavin was the last person she wanted to look at it! She hurried forward and opened the door. He was standing in front of the painting, his hands in his pockets.

"What are you doing?" she got out.

He didn't move.

"Gavin, you can't just come in here!" she scolded, and moved to put a cloth over the painting.

But with his eyes still on the painting, he put out a hand and stopped her. "This is…" He inhaled deeply. "Breathtaking. I've seen some of your paintings, but you haven't done anything like this before, have you?"

"No, and I don't know where it came from. I'm going to paint over it—something…"

"No!" he called out, his eyes meeting her for first time since she'd entered the room. "Why would you do that?"

"It's just…it's not the kind of thing I paint. Ever."

"It's a kiss."

"I know what I've painted," she said crossly.

"And"—he turned back to look at the canvas again—"the figures look familiar somehow…"

Brooke quickly covered the painting with the cloth. "You can barely make out the figures. Come on, the coffee should be ready by now."

She walked down the stairs, acutely aware of Gavin

right behind her. As they entered the kitchen, his phone rang.

"It's Lindsay," he said. News sure did travel fast in this town. "Hi Lindsay," he answered, his lips twitching.

Brooke rolled her eyes. Of course, his other sister would've also heard by now Gavin was with Brooke. Nothing stayed a secret for long. Not that it was a secret... Swallowing a groan, she averted her eyes. She didn't need family members to drive her crazy; she was doing that all on her own.

Damn interfering family. While Gavin was listening to Lindsay, she poured the coffee and put it on the kitchen table. The sooner Gavin Wilson left for the night, the better.

Her heart was hammering away, she had difficulty breathing properly, and she was very worried she might just do something she'd regret later.

Like she'd been telling everyone, she and Gavin were friends. *Friends.*

And friends, she should remember, don't have the kind of inappropriate thoughts about each other, like the ones she was entertaining at the moment. Thoughts of kissing him, of touching his broad shoulders, of finding out whether his mouth was... Oh, damn.

It was probably the stupid painting that had set all these strange feelings inside of her in motion. She had to change it into something different, a calming landscape scene, as soon as possible. It wasn't something she did often, but she'd done it before. She was a widow; she had a child and a demanding career. Her life was busy and complicated enough at the moment. She didn't need other distractions.

"Yes, I'm still here," Gavin's voice finally penetrated her thoughts.

She looked up quickly. He was still talking to Lindsay on the phone.

He was grinning. "I suppose Charlie has phoned you?"

Fed up with the whole situation, Brooke marched

toward Gavin and again grabbed his phone from his hand.

"Lindsay, seriously. Gavin and I are friends. You do know men and women are sometimes just friends?"

"Maybe, but the two of you? I don't think so." Lindsay laughed. "You make such a cute couple. Think how absolutely lovely it would if the two of you get married. Oh, and think of all the cousins playing together on the ranch."

"Lindsay!" Brooke tried to stop her, but she was on a roll.

"We could take turns dropping the kids off at school and, bonus—you won't ever have to worry about cooking again. Gavin, as you would've discovered tonight, is a great cook, don't you think?"

"I'm giving the phone back to Gavin; it's no use talking to you!" Groaning out loud, Brooke handed Gavin's phone back to him before she pulled out a chair and sat down at the table. The whole family was driving her bonkers. Her mother was bad enough on her own. Now that Charlie and Lindsay were teaming up with her, the situation was becoming unbearable.

"I'll talk to you later, Lindsay. Got to go," Gavin finally said and ended the call. He picked up his mug but didn't sit down. Instead, he leaned against the kitchen counter. He sipped his coffee, staring at her. After long minutes, he finally spoke. "So how do we put a stop to this?"

"I suggest we just ignore it. Hopefully, it'll blow over soon."

"You think so?"

"Well, what else do you suggest? Fake a relationship to make them happy?" She didn't even try to cover up the sarcasm.

Slowly, he put his mug down, his eyes never leaving hers. "You know, that's not a bad idea."

Exasperated, she jumped up. "I was being sarcastic! It's a ridiculous idea. We're not...we're just friends. Period."

He crossed his arms. "Think about it. Logan and I are

going to take turns to be at the office in Seattle. It just so happens that I'm leaving for Seattle in two weeks' time. I'll probably stay there for about a month. So, my suggestion is we fake a relationship for the next two weeks, and when I leave, we tell everyone we've ended the relationship amicably, that we're just not a match, and life goes on. That way we get everyone off our backs. The fact that I'll be away for a month also means there will be no awkward moments for you afterwards. By the time I get back from Seattle, everyone will hopefully have forgotten about our relationship, and we can go back to being friends without having to keep explaining that to everyone."

Her mouth opened and closed a few times before she could manage a sound. "It's ludicrous. I have an exhibition in Seattle in the middle of July, and I have to be there, so your plan can't work. Besides, I don't have time for this, I have a million things—"

"Exactly. You have paintings to finish for your exhibition, your mum tells me, and aren't you moving to the farm next week? I can help you with that, help with Connor while you get on with your work. How much time are you going to spend in Seattle?"

"With an exhibition, I usually stay for a few days…"

"We simply tell everyone we're over, and you carry on with your exhibition. I'll be staying in Logan's apartment, though."

"Don't worry about it. I was going to make alternative arrangements closer to the gallery anyway. There is a small Airbnb in downtown Seattle I often use. It's close to the gallery, just a block away. I walk wherever I need to be."

"Then it's settled. After our breakup, we'll tell everyone it didn't work out, and we carry on as friends as we've been doing these past few months."

"It's so silly. You…we can't have a relationship, we're like…like brother and sister!"

He was in her bubble before she'd finished speaking. Slowly, he lifted his hand, cupped her face. "Just for the record—what I feel when I'm around you, can in no way be described as brotherly."

"What...what are you doing?"

"I'm going to kiss you. Two reasons: one, I've been thinking about it all night, and two, then we'll know." By the time he'd finished speaking, his lips were trailing down her face.

She caught her breath. "Know what?" she whispered, unsure of what she was asking.

"Whether we can pretend to be more than friends."

His lips had reached her ear. Desperately, she tried to stay focused, but her eyes closed, sending her other senses into overdrive. The subtle scent of sandalwood seeped through every pore of her body, the sound of his uneven breathing left goosebumps all over her skin, and the feel of his stubble against her cheek had her blood roaring in her ears.

And then his lips touched hers—just briefly before he lifted his head again. Those impossible blue eyes were looking right into her soul.

"What do you think?" he asked.

"What do you mean?" Was the husky voice hers?

"I mean," he said, pulling her closer, "do you think we'll succeed in pretending to be a couple?"

Before her muddled brain could make sense of his words, his warm, wet mouth was on hers again. Oh, my goodness, the man knew how to kiss. She caught her breath; his tongue quickly plunged into her mouth to where her own was eagerly waiting.

Before she realized what she was doing, her hands were on his torso, enthusiastically stroking his muscles before she slipped her arms around his unfamiliar body, exploring his broad shoulders and reveling in the feel of him. She hadn't been this near to a man since Adam...

She was a widow and had no business kissing another man.

Bewildered, she dropped her arms and stepped back.

For a moment, Gavin looked as stunned as she was feeling. He rubbed his face. "That…I didn't expect that. I haven't been with someone for a while."

Brooke nodded and tried a smile. "I haven't been with someone either, since my husband died. That's probably why we've nearly, well, combusted."

Gavin looked incredulous. "You haven't been with anyone? What is wrong with the men in this town? You're so beautiful."

Wow. No man had called her beautiful in quite that tone of voice since… Well, never. Adam had loved her, she'd never doubted that, but he hadn't been one for corny lines or frilly words.

"Don't be silly." She laughed. "I'm a mess. Look at my hair." She combed it back with her fingers. "Frumpy is probably a more accurate description. Anyway, pretending to be a couple is a preposterous idea."

Gavin lifted a hand and touched her face—just briefly, but she felt the touch right down to the very core of her being. "You're gorgeous, whatever state your hair is in." He bent down. "Let me just check if we haven't been mistaken." And then he kissed her again.

This time the kiss just about threw her off her feet, and she had to cling to him to stay upright.

He slowly lifted his head. "I think we could be quite convincing. What do you think?"

The fogginess in her mind finally cleared, and she stepped back quickly. "Forget about it. I've had my chance at love. Adam and I were very happy, and I certainly have no intention of ever getting married again."

"Neither have I. My last girlfriend would be all too willing to tell you how hopeless I am at any kind of relationship, so I know for sure I'm not marriage material. But don't you see? This is exactly why this could work. Neither one of us is interested in anything more permanent. A fake relationship is the perfect way to get our families off our backs."

Chewing her lips, she stared at him. It made sense. It was really getting so boring to keep explaining to everyone that she and Gavin were just friends. It was such a bizarre idea, it might just work.

Gavin groaned and she looked up at him. He was staring at her mouth.

"If you keep doing that, I'll have to kiss you again."

Her mouth was suddenly dry and she slipped out her tongue to wet her lips. He pulled her close. "This...this drives me crazy," he whispered before his mouth descended on hers again.

By now she knew what was coming, but she was still unprepared for the sheer joy streaking through her body. She shouldn't be doing this—she'd been married—she'd loved her husband. Besides, she wasn't a giddy teenager anymore—she had responsibilities—things she should be doing.

But instead of listening to her brain and pushing him away, her hands grabbed hold of his shirt, and she lifted herself on her toes. Desire had her reeling, and getting closer to him was her only goal. He angled his head, deepened the kiss, and oh, my. Were her toes actually curling?

From far away, the sound of a phone ringing penetrated her befuddled brain, but she ignored it. She wasn't ready to give up this moment of bliss just yet. He pulled her close, the heat of his throbbing desire pressed invitingly against her body. Oh. My.

Gavin was the one who finally lifted his head. His eyes were sapphires, liquid with want, his face slightly flushed.

"Your phone is on the table," he muttered before he dropped his hands.

Blindly, she turned around and reached out to pick up her phone. As usual, she hadn't remembered where she'd put it. It was her mother calling, but before she could answer, the ringing stopped. Thank goodness.

Taking a deep breath, she grabbed onto the chair to

steady herself. "That," she said without turning back to him, "can never happen again."

It was quiet behind her, and after a few moments, she twisted around to face Gavin. He was bent slightly forward, still breathing hard.

"Did you hear me?"

"Yeah, I heard you."

"You have to go. Now."

"Just give me a minute, damn it." He adjusted his pants.

Startled, she dropped her gaze to below his middle. Oh. Her eyes flew up to meet his.

He didn't look particularly happy about his body's response. "Yeah. That's why I need a minute."

She needed more than just a minute. Her own body was still humming, her breasts heavy with need. A hysterical giggle threatened to erupt. Swallowing desperately, she tried to keep it way down; this was so not the time to laugh. But the next minute, a laugh slipped out.

"So you think this is funny?" Gavin growled.

"It is kinda funny," she got out in between more stuttering laughs.

Gavin approached her with a light in his eyes, one she recognized by now.

Swallowing the giggles, she put up her hand. "No, stay over there. No more kissing. If you want to do this pretend thing, we'll have to have rules. No touching or kissing."

By the time she'd finished talking, he was right in front of her. "Rules? You? Seriously?"

She swallowed. "Uhm...yes."

"So I can't do this?" His mouth trailed down her face again.

"No." It was barely a whisper.

"Or this?" His mouth lingered on hers for a moment.

She shook her head.

With his eyes on hers, he brushed the backs of his

hands against her aching nipples. "So I assume this is definitely against the rules?"

Her heart skidded to a stop before it valiantly tried to resume beating. She grabbed both of his hands in hers. "We've established neither one of us wants a relationship, so if this pretend-relationship thing is going to work, you…we can't do this."

"Okay." He dropped his hands and turned away. "If that's what you want." He picked up his car keys and walked toward the front door. She followed slowly, taking in the precise detail of how perfectly his jeans stretched across…

"That is not helping."

Her eyes flew up to his. He'd turned around and caught her staring. Face flaming, she pointed toward the door. "Just…go. Please?"

He flashed her a grin, and her knees wobbled. Seriously.

"Just for the record, I'm all for a fake relationship with benefits. We're obviously both sex-starved. Let me know when you change your mind; I'm quite happy to oblige."

She inhaled sharply. "I'm not sex-starved!"

"Wanna test that?" he asked, and gave a step in her direction.

Quickly she held up her hand again. "Go, please. Just…go."

He was still chuckling when she slammed the door shut behind him.

Upset, she crossed her arms. What was so damn funny?

She marched back to the kitchen but once there, she stopped. What had she wanted to do? With a groan, she sat down and dropped her head in her hands.

Sex-starved, Gavin had called them. He was probably right, but she'd never… Shaking her head, she got up quickly. She'd loved her husband; what she was feeling now, was ridiculous.

Her toes had never, ever curled when Adam had kissed

her, a little voice whispered.

Groaning out loud, she leaned back in the chair. She'd never felt like this before. Should she feel guilty? She'd loved Adam; she'd been faithful to him always. But he was gone and this… Grimacing, she got up quickly. This was not real. There was a painting she had to change; she didn't have time to sit around and think about kissing Gavin Wilson.

CHAPTER 3

What the hell had happened last night? It was early morning and Gavin walked out on the back porch with his steaming mug of coffee. In the distance, the Crazy, Absaroka, and Bridger Mountains rose majestically up against a perfect, blue Montana sky.

He'd never even thought of leaving South Africa, but when his sisters had moved to Alisson, Montana about three years before, and Sarah had broken off their relationship, or whatever it had been, he'd realized there was nothing keeping him in his home country any longer. Add to that the increasing violence and corruption that seemed to have taken over South Africa, and it hadn't been a difficult decision to make.

Over the past few months, he'd fallen in love with the wide, open spaces, the fierce mountains, and the gentle, rolling landscapes one finds on the eastern side of Montana.

And the people. The residents of Alisson didn't warm to strangers quickly, but because of his two sisters, he felt tolerated if not quite accepted yet. He'd settled in nicely, loved being close to Charlie and Lindsay, and he was looking forward to his move to the ranch soon. Both he and Blake, Lindsay's husband, had bought shares in Logan's ranch.

But then last night happened. Oh, he'd been aware of Brooke Johnson since day one. The tall widow, with her honey-blond hair and blue eyes, was gorgeous, and yes, he also noticed those gorgeous long legs that seemed to go on forever. But up 'til now, he'd studiously ignored the fist of desire he experienced every time he saw her. Apart from the fact that he wasn't interested in a relationship, everyone still talked about Brooke's late husband Adam and how happy the two of them had been.

But then, yesterday, he'd opened his front door to find her son on his porch, asking him to please cook for them. That single incident had been the trigger for everything that had happened last night.

He should've listened to his gut and found some or other excuse, but apart from the fact that he couldn't say no to that pleading pair of blue eyes, so much like the mother's, he was intrigued. For the first time, he had a legitimate reason to visit the lovely widow without any of his sisters around.

The rest of the evening he couldn't have planned even if he'd tried. Brooke was the one who'd mentioned a "fake relationship." At the time it had sounded like a good idea. But that was before he'd kissed her.

There was nothing "fake" about the way his body reacted to the kiss, to her. He couldn't remember ever getting that turned on that quickly. And what was driving him crazy was the fact that she'd responded to him as passionately.

His phone bleeped. It was a message. From the lovely Brooke, no less.

We have to talk. Set our stories straight. Sign a contract.

By the time he'd finished reading, he was grinning. Brooke Johnson was your typical artist who mostly lived in a world of her own, where ordinary things—like being on time, knowing where her phone, keys, bag were, eating at specific times—were not important. And now she wanted to "set their stories straight" and heaven forbid, "sign a contract."

This, he had to see.

Brooke was pacing the part of the corridor right in front of the front door. She stopped and listened. No, it wasn't Gavin's car yet. She had so much work to do, but she had to talk to him before she'd be able to do any of it.

She hadn't slept a wink last night, and the few times she had managed to drift away, steamy scenes of entwined bodies had woken her up. Her heart would be racing, her body ready to...well, to make love.

Since Adam had passed away three years ago, the last thing on her mind had been sex. She had their little boy to look after. It had also been around the same time the gallery in Missoula had seen her work on social media and had asked if they could represent her. They'd organized an exhibition, leading to more work. Not that she was complaining—she loved what she was doing—but there simply wasn't time in her day for kissing, let alone sex.

Sex? Upset, she rubbed her face. Why was she still thinking about sex? Gavin had said they were both sex-starved. Maybe he wasn't that far wrong. Maybe that was the reason for the painting, the reason why she was now in this ridiculous situation. Maybe—

The doorbell chimed.

Brooked stopped pacing and stared at the door. *He's here.* On the other side of her front door. Why on earth had she invited him over? She could've sent him an email with the contract or something, or even just texted him. He didn't have to come to her house. There were other ways.

The doorbell chimed again. Taking a deep breath, she rubbed her suddenly clammy hands against her jeans before she opened the door. He turned to look at her, his light brown hair windblown, his blue eyes filled with a light that had her knees do that silly wobbling thing again.

"Brooke. You mentioned a contract?"

She opened the door wider. This had been such a bad idea. They were all alone; Connor was still at school. What had she been thinking, for crying out loud? She hadn't been thinking, that was the problem. At least not clearly. She still had brain fog after last night's scrumptious kisses… Oh, damn, she shouldn't be thinking about last night's kisses!

"If you keep looking at me like that, I'll have to kiss you again," Gavin said, his voice hoarse.

Face flaming, she turned away and marched toward the kitchen. She'd been staring at his mouth. The same mouth that had kissed her last night. The mouth she'd been dreaming about throughout the night.

The "contract" she'd been working on since the crack of dawn was lying on the table, and she quickly picked it up. "No kissing… Look, it's point number one."

Gavin took the piece of paper from her and leaned against the kitchen cupboard. He began reading what she'd typed.

He was here, in her house, and all she could think about was how his lips had felt against her, how perfectly she'd fitted against his body, how…

Inhaling slowly, she tried to calm down her wayward thoughts. Damn, this had to be one of the stupidest things she'd ever done, and that was saying a lot. She tended to do silly things—her mind was mostly on her paintings and not on everyday things. But this particular, everyday thing, she should have given it more thought. Much more thought.

Before either one of them could speak, someone knocked on the front door. The next minute she heard her mother. "Anybody home? Brooke? Is Gavin's car still…?" Her mother appeared in the kitchen door, wearing one of her Pilates outfits.

Her gaze moved between the two of them. Her mouth fell open, her eyes widened, and then she clapped her hands. "Oh, you two! I knew if you spent time together, you'd realize you were absolutely meant for each other. I had to come and see for myself. I had just driven into town when Cynthia Higgins called me. Gavin's car was still in front of Brooke's house, she told me. I couldn't believe it. Of course, I mean, you keep insisting you're just friends, but look at the two of you!"

Brooke groaned out loud. "Mom…"

But before Brooke could utter another word, Gavin had moved closer and put his arm around her. "We were going to announce it tonight with a dinner at a restaurant, but yes, we're together. And you're absolutely right. Last night we realized we're much more than just friends. You want to tell her, babe?"

Brooke stiffened. *Babe?* Where did that come from? But with her mother's gaze following them as if she was watching a tennis match, Brooke couldn't say or do anything else but smile. "We've…" What on earth was she supposed to say?

Gavin kissed her temple. "Don't be shy, babe. Surely you can tell your mother?"

He was enjoying this—*look at his grin*. Well, two could play this game. She slid her hand up his torso, and batting her eyelashes, she looked up at him. "He kissed me, Mom. A toe-curling one, I must add. So what was a girl to do but kiss him back?"

Gavin's eyes narrowed slightly, but below her fingers his heart was hammering away like a freight train. Mmm, not nearly so calm and collected as he would have her thinking.

Her mother sighed, clearly in rapture. "Oh, how romantic!"

"And does he know how to kiss?" Brooke sighed dramatically and let her fingers glide ever so slightly over Gavin's bottom lip.

As he inhaled softly, his eyes darkened. She caught her breath and quickly dropped her hand. Oh, my. Her only thought had been to punish him for blurting out their relationship to her mother, of all people. They still had things to discuss, a contract to sign. The last thing she wanted to do was to unleash more sexual tension, but now she could swear the air around them was literally vibrating.

She gave a cursory glance around her. Where was the contract?

Tears were streaming down her mom's face. "Oh, my darling girl, I'm so, so happy for you!" She threw her arms around them both. "I knew it, I knew it," she repeated over and over.

"Okay, Mom, stop crying, please?" Brooke felt awful. Lying had never done anyone any good. Her mother would be devastated when they eventually had to tell her they were breaking up.

"Happy tears, my dear girl, happy tears!" Her mom already had her phone out, the tears forgotten. "I have to go. I can't wait to tell Charlie and Lindsay! Our usual restaurant? At seven?"

But she wasn't really interested in any answers; she was already heading toward the front door, her phone against her ear.

The moment Brooke heard the front door close behind her mother, she rounded on Gavin. "See what you've done? Before night falls, she's going to have our whole wedding planned out, mark my words. You're going to be paying for the flowers and a wedding cake, and she'll have you buy a ring before you know what hit you."

She began pacing again. "We haven't thought this through. Oh, I like your kisses, toe-curling as I've said, but what about Connor? He's desperate for a father figure in his life, and he already likes you. How will he handle our fake relationship? What do we tell him and what happens when we break up?" Out of breath, she finally stopped pacing and looked at Gavin.

He was staring at her.

She threw up her arm. "Great. You're already sorry about the whole mess. Well, unless you run after my mother and stop her from telling another soul, everyone in Alisson will know we're a couple before night falls."

"So you like my kisses? Toe-curling, you call them."

Brooked opened and closed her mouth a few times before she could string words together. "That's all you got, from everything else I've said?"

He approached her slowly. "You haven't answered my question. You liked my kisses?" By the time he'd finished speaking, they were toe to toe.

She rolled her eyes. "Seriously? We have things to discuss, a contract to sign… Where is the contract, by the way?"

"I'll answer your question when you answer mine."

She threw both her hands in the air. "Yes, damn it, I liked your kisses. I dreamed about your kisses. Hap—?"

His mouth was on hers before she could finish speaking. His lips were warm and urgent. Within seconds, a wild torrent of passion nearly lifted her off her feet. In a desperate attempt to stay upright, she grabbed hold of his arms, but that was a mistake. Beneath her fingers, hard muscles rippled, making her already heated blood nearly boiling hot.

She shouldn't be doing this. Kissing Gavin Wilson was such a bad idea. Enjoying Gavin Wilson's kissing was an even worse one, but how did she stop this when it felt so incredibly right? Right?

Whoa.

With superhuman effort, she pulled back. They were both panting.

Quickly, she moved away and turned her back on Gavin. "That… I told you that can't happen again!" She had difficulty getting the words out.

For long minutes, all she could hear was his heavy breathing. Or was it hers?

"Can I tell you what I think of your so-called contract?"

She turned to face him again. "You were the one who thought faking a relationship was a good idea. I agreed, but with conditions—"

He swore. Her eyes widened. She'd never heard him swear before.

Slowly, he advanced while pulling something out of the pocket of his jeans. It was the contract. He ripped it in four pieces. "This is what I think of you so-called contract. We're both adults. We're both single. Neither one of us wants this relationship to last more than a few weeks. But I can't touch you and not kiss you, as your contracted stipulated. And you see, babe, I am going to touch you. I want to touch you. When I'm around you, that's all I can think of. Not sure how much clearer I can make myself."

He was pulling her closer. Desperately, she tried to remember all the reasons why she shouldn't be doing this. "I've been married already…"

"Do you think I don't know that? You've been with someone else, not something I like to think about. But this here, is us. And I'm the one holding you, I'm the one kissing you, don't forget that." His mouth claimed hers again, wiping out all objections.

Within seconds, a whirlwind picked her up again, and she spun out of control. She grabbed onto Gavin's shirt in an effort to steady herself, but the warmth of his body penetrated her skin through the T-shirt he was wearing, and her heart simply took over the workings of her brain. She happily leaned into the kiss.

There was no way she could ever mistake his kisses with anyone else's.

The hysterical voice, trying to warn him to stop, finally penetrated the haze of lust that had Gavin reeling. Out of breath, he lifted his head. He didn't remember doing it, but his hands had found their way underneath Brooke's top and were caressing satiny skin.

Brooke's blue eyes were nearly black with desire.

"Damn, babe, you're killing me," he murmured, resting his forehead against hers.

"I had a contract…"

He swore again. "No contract, signed or otherwise, will keep me from wanting to kiss you, to touch you, damn it."

She pulled herself out of his arms and began pacing. Her hair had slipped out of the ponytail again, her face was still slightly flushed, her lips swollen from his kisses. He pushed his hands into the pockets of his jeans. Everything inside him was urging him to pick her up, carry her upstairs, and make love to her until neither of them could see straight.

But if he did that, he wouldn't be able to let her go. Ever. And that wasn't something that could happen, was it?

Brooke was frantically looking around her. "Where is my phone? I have to stop my mom from telling everyone else…"

Gavin's phone started ringing. "Too late. It's Charlie."

Brooke threw her hands in the air. "That's great. Just great!"

"Hi, sis."

"You're with Brooke!" Charlie shrieked. "Oh, I'm so, so happy for you, Gavin. So happy!"

His sister was just about yelling. Flinching, Gavin held the phone away from his ear and put it on speaker.

"Thank you," he began.

But his sister was on a roll and not at all interested in anything he had to say. "We've just spoken to Eleanor— Lindsay's here with me. We were wondering if you'd mind if we have dinner here on the ranch? Linds and I will cook. It's just easier with Ellie. Shall we say six o'clock? Tell Brooke Connor can sleep over; Lindsay says Blake will be going into town quite early tomorrow and he can drop him off at school. That'll give you two lovebirds some alone-time. Oooh—we're so, so happy! See you later."

Gavin put his phone away and walked toward the side cupboard where Brooke's phone lay. He picked it up and handed it to her. "Here. Still want to call your mother?"

Clearly irritated, Brooke grabbed it from him. "I would've found my own damn phone, thank you. There will be no point in calling my mom now. By this time, she's already told everyone in town." She was chewing her lip again; his eyes followed every single movement. "Okay, we do this for two weeks, but you can't…"

He pulled her closer and cupped her face. "I'm going to kiss you, Brooke, and often. Get used to it." His lips hovered over hers. He had to be sure. "Do you know who's going to kiss you now?"

Her eyes were on his lips. "My toes have never curled before…"

That was all he needed to hear. His mouth slid over hers, capturing her bottom lip between his, desire slamming into his gut. She was soft and warm, and within seconds, he was feasting on her full mouth, inhaling her unique scent of orange blossom and something he couldn't quite distinguish. This was what had been driving him crazy since day one.

His hands roamed over her back, quickly finding their way back under her top. Skin on skin. Satin. Velvet. Soft. So soft he could spend days exploring every centimeter. But he wanted to have more of her. So much more.

He eased back, lifting his head slowly. "I want you. So badly," he whispered, his desire for her throbbing painfully between them.

The embers of passion were still burning in her eyes, but she stepped back, gulping in air. "See? That's what happens when you kiss me! I forget about everything else." Her eyes widened. I…I can't believe I've just told you that. The point is, we can't kiss—"

"We're going to kiss, babe, that's not negotiable."

"So what happens after two weeks?"

"I won't be here. I'll be in Seattle. By that time, whatever fire we've lit between the two of us will be extinguished and we'll move on."

She stared at him, again chewing her lower lip. The one he'd had between his own lips. His body reacted.

"Okay," she finally said. "Kissing is allowed. But that's it. No touching of body parts underneath our clothes."

"Seriously?"

"Seriously. I don't sleep around."

He wanted to pull her close and kiss her until she begged him to take off every piece of her clothing, but she was right. He didn't like it, but he couldn't promise her a happy-ever-after, and she had been very clear about the fact she wasn't getting married again. Besides, he would probably be the one doing the begging.

He nodded. "If that's what you want."

"That's what I want."

"I don't have the same stipulations. So if…" He couldn't help himself, he had to touch her face again. "If you change your mind, you know where to find me." And ignoring the loud voice in his head, he bent down and kissed the side of her mouth before he turned around and walked out of her kitchen.

If she were to call him back, he wouldn't be responsible for what happened next.

CHAPTER 4

Thank goodness for Connor. Brooke turned around in the car and smiled at her son, who was sitting in the back seat of Gavin's car. Connor had been chatting nonstop ever since they'd left Alisson to drive to the ranch for dinner. She'd never been more grateful for his running commentary on everything he saw outside the car. Neither she nor Gavin had said anything yet.

She'd wanted to meet Gavin on the ranch, but he'd pointed out that since they were now "together," everyone would expect him to drive her and Connor there. Although she didn't like it, it made sense and she had to agree. However, she wasn't going to leave Connor behind tonight, no matter what her mom had said. About her reasons for doing so, she didn't want to think too much.

Letting Gavin walk out of her house that morning had been very, very difficult. Her whole being wanted to be with him, to make love with him, to become a part of him. She had no idea where this...lust had come from, suddenly.

Two days ago, Gavin had just been her brother's brother-in-law. Okay, her brother's very sexy, very attractive brother-in-law, but she'd managed to keep her distance. And then Connor had brought him home to cook for them, they'd concocted this bizarre plan of pretending to have a relationship to get their families off their backs—and now, everything had changed.

No, that hadn't been the reason for the change. The main reason, if she were to be brutally honest, was the kiss. Her toes curled, for goodness' sake. Wasn't she too old for that? And not just once. She'd allowed Gavin to kiss her four times. Or was it five? One thing was clear, though— she wasn't thinking straight. Was this because she was—to use Gavin's word—sex-starved?

Whatever the reason, she wasn't thinking straight, she wasn't sleeping properly—the worst combination when she was supposed to be painting.

"Relax," Gavin said, picking up her hand.

"Relax? How can I relax?" she whispered. "I still haven't told Connor. I'm not sure what to tell him. And what happens when…?"

"So let's tell him. Together."

"But what do I say?"

"We'll wing it. Hey, Connor?"

"Yes, Gavin?"

"Your mom and I are going to spend more time together. Would that be okay for you?"

For a few moments it was quiet in the car. Brooke wanted to throttle Gavin. She should've prepared Connor, she knew, but she hadn't expected Gavin to blurt out the whole thing like that. This fake-relationship thing had to be one of the worst decisions she'd ever made.

"Does it mean you'll be cooking for us?" Connor finally asked.

Gavin laughed. "Yes, exactly. It also means"—he glanced sideways at Brooke and winked—"I'll be kissing your mom from time to time."

Brooke's heart nearly jumped out of her throat, and she glared at Gavin. Why did he have to talk about kissing her, to her son of all people, for crying out loud?

"Ew, gross," Connor said. "Why do you have to do that?"

"Well, I like her, you see, and when you like someone, you like to kiss them sometimes."

Brooke turned to talk to Connor. This whole thing was crazy. The sooner she put an end to it, the better for all of them. Connor was staring out of the window.

"Connor, sweetheart…"

"Mom kisses me all the time."

Gavin grinned. "That's because she really, really likes you."

"Do you really, really like my mom?" Connor asked.

"I do. I really, really like her," Gavin said.

"Okay," Connor nodded. "Are we there yet?"

"Nearly."

Connor began chatting about what he was going to do on the farm once they got there, talk of kissing all forgotten. Brooke exhaled slowly. This whole thing was spiraling out of control—she hated the feeling. Hadn't she promised herself she'd never be in a situation again where she wasn't in charge? But look at her. She had agreed to a fake relationship, of all things. She wasn't even in charge of her own feelings, damn it. She should never have agreed; the whole idea was preposterous.

"It's two weeks, babe," Gavin said softly. "You're going to be busy, and I can help you with Connor over the coming weekend. He loves spending time on the ranch. We'll have a great time while you work."

Irritated, she glared at him. "You don't have to organize my life for me. I'm quite capable of doing that all by myself, thank you."

Gavin grinned. "I know. I'm simply offering to help." He glanced in the rear-view mirror. "When do schools close, Connor?"

"Friday!" Connor yelled. "And Saturday is my birthday."

Brooke couldn't help smiling. Connor was so excited

about his upcoming birthday. "No, sweetie, your birthday is only next Saturday. Hopefully, by that time, we'd have moved into our house on the ranch."

"Am I also invited?" Gavin asked.

"Can you barbeque?" Connor asked.

Gavin chuckled. "Back in South Africa we call it a 'braai,' and like any South African male, I learned to braai pretty much before I could walk."

"Great! Because Mom...well, last time we had a barbeque, she burned the patties and we only had rolls."

Gavin laughed, squeezing her hand.

Brooke's face instantly went red. "It wasn't that bad; you don't have to give up your Saturday to—"

But Gavin interrupted her with a laugh. "I don't mind."

"Thank you!" Connor called out dramatically.

"So what about I come and pick you up this Saturday, Connor?" Gavin asked. "You and I can check on the progress of your house."

"Can I, Mom?"

"May I," she corrected him automatically. "I don't think we should bother Gavin..."

But Connor was bouncing enthusiastically up and down. "I can't wait to play with Bear and Sasha and Lucy."

"I'm glad you're not afraid of the dogs." Gavin smiled.

"They're my friends," Connor said. "Oh, and I love the horses. The black one is my favorite. Blake said..."

As Connor chatted away, Brooke hardly registered what her son was saying. Her eyes were on her hand lying contentedly in Gavin's. If she didn't watch her poor heart, she was going to get into real trouble. She tried to pull her hand away, but Gavin held on tightly.

"No touching, remember?" she whispered.

"You said no touching beneath clothes—this doesn't count." And then he lifted her hand and kissed her fingers, a touch she felt right down to her very core. Oh, my. They had to make more rules, set more boundaries...

She swallowed the half-hysterical giggle threatening to

erupt. Making rules, setting boundaries were so not how she lived her life. She wouldn't even know how to go about doing that. The "contract" she'd drawn up was lying in tatters in the wastepaper basket, a clear indication of her lack of power to do anything within boundaries.

"Are we there yet?" Connor whined again.

"A few minutes more," Gavin said. "We're nearly there."

They'd reached the huge gate at the entrance of the ranch, and were on the road leading up to the homestead. Inhaling deeply, Brooke frantically tried to calm herself. Within minutes, her mother would see her, and Mom never missed a thing. With a soft gasp, she tried to steady her breathing before she hyperventilated.

Setting boundaries and taking charge of her life would have to wait for later that night.

"Can we go and look at our house while we're here, Mom?" Connor wanted to know.

"Yes, of course, sweetheart."

Gavin parked in front of the house, and the front door flew open. The two German shepherds, Bear and Sasha, were right in front, tails wagging as they ran down the stairs. From the direction of Lindsay's house, Lucy, the Spaniel Blake had bought for them, also came running toward them, ears flapping.

Charlie and Eleanor were behind them, and Lindsay followed, a little bit slower, her hand protectively on her abdomen.

Eleanor opened her arms and caught Connor as he rushed into her hug while the dogs barked happily. "I'm so happy to see you!"

Brooke was so tense, but she couldn't help laughing. Connor adored his grandma, and even though she wasn't your typical grandma who knitted, cooked, and baked cakes, she had the ability to make every mundane thing exciting.

While Connor went to greet Charlie and Lindsay, her

mom clapped her hands before she hugged Brooke. "We have bubbly on ice. We can't wait to celebrate you two being together. We're all so, so happy for you."

"He says he's going to kiss her," Connor announced.

"Really?" her mother asked, eyes twinkling.

"He says he really, really likes her."

Everyone laughed. Charlie embraced Brooke before she hugged her brother. "I can't tell you how happy we all are about your news. You dark horse, you!"

Lindsay also stepped closer to hug Brooke and her brother. "You two belong together; we've known it for quite some time, now! Come on in. We want all the details. Every single one."

Gavin had Brooke's hand in his as they stepped onto the back porch. A long table was covered with a white tablecloth and festively set. Logan and Blake looked up from where they were busy with drinks. Connor was kicking a ball on the lawn.

Logan's gaze fell on Gavin and Brooke's entwined hands. His eyes narrowed slightly even though his smile stayed in place.

Blake reached them first. "I hear congratulations are in order. Happy for you guys."

"Thank you," Brooke said, and then Logan enveloped her in a hug.

"He messes with you, you tell me," Logan said, his eyes on Gavin.

As Gavin put out his hand to shake Logan's, he tried to prepare himself for the handshake he was about to get. He remembered all too well the hard time he'd given Logan when he couldn't make up his mind about Charlie. Logan was clearly about to reciprocate.

He was right. Logan gripped his hand tightly and squeezed. It took all his self-control not to wince. Okay, he'd deserved it. This time.

"How does your involvement with my sister influence your decision to be in the Seattle office for a month?" Logan asked coolly.

"I'm still going—that's not a problem. Brooke knows about our arrangement, but we haven't discussed details yet. She's preparing for her exhibition and will be working hard, but maybe when she's there for her exhibition, she and Connor could come and stay with me for a few days. We'll see."

Eleanor bustled outside with a bowl of salad in her hands. "Have you popped the bubbly, Logan?"

"On my way, Mom." Logan shot Gavin a last, warning look before he turned back to open the bottle of bubbly.

Well, hell. When Brooke pulled her hand out of his, Gavin let her go. It was one thing to decide to have a "fake" relationship, it was an entirely different exercise to answer all the many questions they didn't really have answers to.

He liked Brooke. He liked touching her; that wasn't the problem. So what was the problem? He gazed around, searching for Brooke even before he realized what he was doing. His two sisters both had their arms around her, and they were all smiling.

Something tightened around his upper body, making it difficult to breathe. This was a temporary arrangement. Once he left for Seattle, they'd tell everyone it had been a mistake, and then they could both hopefully carry on with their lives without the constant winking and nudging from his sisters and Brooke's mom.

Soon everyone had a glass of bubbly in hand, and somehow, without consciously thinking about it, he'd found his way close to Brooke again.

"A toast!" Eleanor was saying, her eyes bright with tears. Everyone lifted their glasses. "To the next wedding!"

Brooke groaned. "Mom, seriously. Nobody is talking about a wedding. We're together—for the moment. That's what we're celebrating."

Eleanor looked over her shoulder, to where Connor was playing on the grass, and dropped her voice. "Okay, but just so you know, Charlie and Lindsay and I have been talking and sooner would be better than later," Brooke's mom said, her eyes shining. "Lindsay is due to give birth in September, and it would be easier all around if we could have you two married and settled before then. It also means it wouldn't be necessary to build another house for you, Gavin."

Next to Gavin, Brooke gasped, while the word "married" exploded in his head.

"Mother!" Brooke called out. "That is so out of line, I don't even know what to say to you."

Nobody was paying any attention to Brooke, though. Charlie grabbed his arm. "Ooh, and Gavin, Lindsay and I have wondered if you still had Mom's ring? You know, the ruby..." Charlie grabbed her mouth and her eyes widened. "Oops, so sorry! Was it supposed to be a surprise?"

Gavin shook his head. It was as if they'd all gotten on a runaway train that was simply going faster and faster, and there wasn't anything he could do to stop it. "I think that's enough interfering for one day, don't you think?"

"Lindsay, how are you feeling?" Brooke asked. It was clear she was trying to change the subject, but whether his sisters and mom would allow it, they'd have to see.

The women moved toward each other, and he followed Blake out onto the lawn, where Connor was still playing. Blake caught the ball and threw it at Gavin, but he was still watching Brooke and was hit in the shoulder.

Blake grinned. "Eyes on the ball. This one we're playing with."

Gavin did his best to focus on the game. For a few minutes, they played with the little boy until Eleanor called everyone to go and wash hands—lunch was ready.

Grinning, Blake slapped him on the shoulder. "You have it bad, my friend. Welcome to the club."

"What club are we talking about?"

"The I-don't-want-to-live-without-her club." Blake rushed forward to help Lindsay into a chair.

Gavin watched the attentive way Blake helped Lindsay. Yeah, he was familiar with the club. He'd seen enough of his sisters and their husbands to know what Blake was talking about. Two days ago, he would've sworn he'd never felt like that about anyone. But after the last two days?

Brooke was also taking her seat, and he hastened forward. If he were to sit next to her, he could touch her whenever he wanted to.

And it would seem he wanted to do that all the time. If he wasn't mistaken, he was in trouble. Deep, deep trouble.

After dinner that night, it was still light enough to walk down to Brooke's nearly finished house. She'd been here a few times before to check on the progress, but she'd been so busy trying to finish paintings before she and Connor moved here permanently, she hadn't been back over the last three weeks.

Gavin was walking next to her, holding her hand as he'd been doing through most of the evening. It was a strange feeling—being touched this way again. She'd missed the intimacy of having a partner; maybe that was why she was so conscious of her hand in Gavin's. It would be so easy to get used to the idea of being with someone again.

Logan moved closer to her. "We have a surprise for you."

Her mom laughed. "I can't wait for you to see what Logan has added. I had to keep it a secret all this time, and you know how hard that is for me."

"Added?" Brooke frowned. "I told you Connor and I don't need a huge house. All I really need is a place near a window where I can paint. And a bed."

Smiling, Logan opened the front door. "We know. But

it was easy to change the plans slightly to make sure you have a big enough place where you can paint. Come and have a look."

Connor raced inside. "It's nearly finished, Mom!" he yelled.

The kitchen, living room, and dining room were one large, open space with big windows facing the mountains. Pulling her hand from Gavin's, she twirled around to get a good look at the whole room. "Wow, Logan, it looks as if you guys are just about done. It's perfect."

"I'm glad you like it." Logan grinned. "Come, your surprise is this way."

She was aware of Gavin following them down a short corridor.

"Your bedroom," Logan said, pointing to the first room, "Connor's room opposite yours and down here"—he opened a door at what was the end of the corridor the last time she was here—"your studio."

"Studio? But I told you…"

Logan grabbed her hand and pulled her into the room. "I know. But it's time for my very talented sister to have her own studio. What do you think?"

Slowly, Brooke turned around, trying to take everything in: The big windows overlooking the mountains would ensure more than enough natural light; two cupboards for all her art supplies; a tiled floor for easy cleaning; and look at all the space—it was double the size of her bedroom. In her mind's eye, she was already unpacking her art supplies and placing her easel in front of the window just so, to catch the last of the light.

She threw her arms around Logan's neck, tears running over her face. "It's perfect. Just perfect."

Her brother laughed and hugged her as the rest of the party also entered the big room. Gavin was standing slightly to the side, a strange expression on his face. Before she could move toward him, though, his sisters rushed forward.

"You like it?" Charlie wanted to know.

"I love it." Brooke smiled. "But the extra cost…"

Logan smiled. "It's our pleasure to give you and Mom the studios you deserve."

Her mom was crying and laughing at the same time. "Oh, I'm so happy! Not only are you moving to the ranch soon, but we'll be working near each other again, and I can look forward to another wedding and many more babies now that you and Gavin…"

"Mom!" Brooke groaned. "We're together, that's it. Nobody is talking about a wedding and babies."

"But that would be the next step, surely?"

"Can we please just enjoy the moment?" Brooke smiled, her eyes searching for Gavin.

But he wasn't around. He'd found a way to keep touching her all throughout the long day; it felt strange not to have him close by. She quickly turned back to the others. What was she thinking? Nothing about her and Gavin was real.

She needed to remember that.

CHAPTER 5

The whole reason Brooke hadn't wanted Connor to stay behind on the ranch after dinner was because she didn't want to be alone with Gavin when he dropped her off. There, she'd finally allowed herself to acknowledge the real reason.

When Connor had fallen asleep on Charlie and Logan's sofa, her mom had suggested he spend the night there even though she hadn't brought his pajamas or a clean set of clothes, as she would've have done if she'd thought to leave him behind. Brooke had used that as an excuse to insist he went home with her. And before she could do it, Gavin had picked him up and carried him to the car.

By the time Gavin was driving into Alisson, it was nearly ten and dark outside. She'd just realized her plan wasn't working out quite as she'd thought it would. They were, for all purposes, alone. Connor was fast asleep, and as she knew all too well that he wouldn't wake up for anything at this stage.

She looked down at her hand in Gavin's. When they'd driven away from the farm, he'd again picked it up, and he hadn't dropped it since. It was a short trip from the ranch, but it had felt like hours. Where their hands touched, her skin was hot, burning.

Gavin had been silent since they'd all visited her nearly finished house. Something was obviously bothering him, but with the rising sexual tension in the car, it was hard to think about anything else.

She was conscious of Gavin's every move next to her, of his breathing, his smell, his warm hand covering hers. Hot flames were licking her insides, making it difficult to breathe.

When he stopped in front of her house, she was out of the door before he had a chance to open his. She had to get away from him before she did something stupid.

Gavin climbed out slowly, his gaze meeting hers across the car. "I'll take Connor in."

Normally she would've insisted to carry Connor by herself, but the sooner they had Connor in bed, the sooner Gavin could leave.

She walked ahead of him, unlocked the door, switched on lights, and ran up the stairs to make sure Connor's bed was ready.

Her heart was beating frantically, the blood was pounding in her ears, her mouth was bone dry, her body was heavy, hot with need. Gavin had to leave as soon as possible, otherwise she might just forget about all her rules, and jump his bones. Oh, my goodness, she shouldn't even be thinking about jumping and his bones: as it was, her blood was close to boiling.

Gavin was right behind her, and he put Connor down on the bed. His movements were so gentle, she had to swallow the lump in her throat. She pulled the blankets over Connor and without looking in Gavin's direction, hurried out of the room and down the stairs.

"Thank you," she said stiffly and walked toward the front door.

Gavin was right behind her. "Brooke."

She was forced to look up to him. "Yes?"

He caught her hand in his.

"Gavin…" Her mouth was so dry, though, she couldn't get another word out.

"Do you want me to leave?"

She stared at him, chewing her lip. That would be the sensible thing to do. She knew it. Her breasts felt heavy with want, and desire was a throbbing ache all over her body.

With a growl, he bent forward and kissed her. "It drives me wild when you do that." He cupped her face. "I'll leave if that's what you want."

Slowly, she shook her head. "It's not what I want, but we have to talk about bound—"

He kissed her again. "The time for boundaries is long gone, babe. No buts. Yes or no. I'll respect your decision." He dropped his hands.

"You should go," she pleaded. "I'm…burning up."

Something flashed in his eyes. "And you think telling me that helps?"

She hugged herself. "This is crazy. You know it. You're leaving in two weeks' time. You don't really want this. As we've established yesterday, we're both…"

"Sex-starved," he said.

"I don't know if I'd describe it quite like that, but okay, yes. Anything more than…kissing will only complicate this whole thing even more."

He exhaled slowly. "Okay, I'll go. So kissing is allowed?"

"It's not a good idea."

His eyes were hot, molten lava. She waited for him to pull her closer, but he turned around and opened the front door. "Okay. But for the record, I don't see why we can't enjoy our time together."

"Because it's not real, remember. That's why it's called a 'fake' relationship."

He turned back quickly and pulled her close. His mouth trailed soft kisses down her face. "What I feel when I'm with you, babe, is very real. There's nothing fake about the way my body responds to you."

His warm desire throbbed against her body. She was just about ready to burst into flames. "Gavin…"

"It's okay. I know I have nothing to offer you that you don't already have. I'm leaving," he got out, his voice not quite steady.

Even before he'd reached his car, she'd closed and locked the door. Not to keep him out, but to keep herself inside the house.

She pressed her ear against it and waited for his car to start. Long seconds ticked by before she heard the soft purr of the engine. Only when it was finally silent outside did she breathe again.

That had been so close. She was shaking with need. Rubbing her face, she walked toward the kitchen. Tea. A whole pot. There wasn't even a remote chance that she'd be able to sleep tonight; she may as well work. She had a week to do the packing for her move to the ranch next week. And there was a painting she had to change.

Halfway through the process of making tea, she stopped. What had Gavin meant when he'd said, 'I have nothing to offer you that you don't already have?'" He'd been strangely quiet after they'd been to her house. Something was bothering him, but what?

Oh, damn, she was still thinking about the man, and he'd left minutes ago.

When Brooke's phone rang late Thursday morning, she was still staring at *The Kiss.* That's what she'd dubbed the painting in her mind, anyway. Since Tuesday night, she'd been trying to change the painting of the two figures kissing, but all she'd succeeded in doing was to add a deeper shade of grey here and there. Her fingers and brush simply ignored any other messages from her brain.

Absentmindedly, she answered her phone. It was Sally Smith, the owner of the gallery in Livingston.

"Brooke, hello. I'm sorry to disturb you, but we have a situation."

Brooked was still staring at the painting, but something in Sally's voice caught her attention. "What situation?"

"We were unable to collect your two paintings from the gallery in Missoula. Bill Norton, the new manager, refused to give them to the movers who went to pick it up this morning."

"But why? I've sent him and Lynda an email…"

"He claims he doesn't know anything about it."

"I don't believe it!" Brooke groaned. She honestly didn't have time for this. "I have new paintings I can bring you, hopefully before I move to the ranch next week," she offered.

"I actually have buyers for those two specific paintings in Missoula," Sally said. "I've advertised the paintings when I've let all my clients know we'll be curating your paintings in future, as well, and I've had quite a few offers…"

Sally's voice droned on, but Brooke wasn't listening anymore. She honestly didn't need an extra complication in her life. Her house looked as if it had been hit by a hurricane. Empty and half-filled boxes were all over the place; she was trying to paint and pack at the same time.

She'd sent the email to Lynda and Bill two days ago, but she hadn't heard from either of them. Lynda, it would seem, was apparently somewhere in the Mediterranean, probably why she hadn't yet heard from her, but Bill Norton had also been quiet. She probably should've checked with him again already, but with all the packing and painting, it had slipped her mind.

After finishing her call with Sally, she tried to call Lynda, but there was only a voicemail message to say she'd be out of reach for the next week.

She tried Bill Norton's phone number. He picked up at the second ring. "Brooke, darling—"

"Why didn't you give my paintings to the movers this

morning? I seriously don't have time for this."

"You can't expect me to hand over precious paintings to some random firm—surely you can understand that?"

Grinding her teeth, she tried to calm down. "I've always done it like this…"

"Well, now things are different. As I've explained to you before, I usually have close relationships with my artists and I can't do that if I never see them."

"First of all, I'm not your anything, and secondly—"

"You want your paintings?" he interrupted her.

"Of course, I do!"

"Well, then, I hope to see you soon!" The next minute, the line was dead.

Stunned, she looked down at her phone. Seriously? Taking a deep breath, she scrolled through her contacts. An attorney. That's what she needed now. She'd phone Guy Richard. He'd been helping her mother with legal stuff for as long as she could remember. He'd also been a big help after Adam had passed away. Hopefully, Guy had an unthreatening way to persuade freaking Bill Norton to ship her paintings to the gallery in Livingston.

Gavin lifted his hand to knock on the door. He dropped it again. What the hell was he doing here, on Brooke's porch in the middle of a Thursday? He had work to do, and as had become clear to him on Tuesday, she didn't need him. She was a famous artist with a brother who could give her everything she needed, including building her a dream studio.

There was nothing he could offer her she didn't already have. But here he was, his heart pounding in his chest because she was on the other side of this door.

He knocked. And waited. He wasn't going to touch her; he just needed to know she was okay. He knocked again. Nothing. Her car was in front of the house, the windows were open, she…

The door flew open and there she was—on the phone, frowning, her hair all over the place. Motioning him inside, she turned away, still talking.

"Thanks, Guy, I can kiss you right now. I so appreciate your help. Thanks again, goodbye."

"Who the hell is Guy and why do you want to kiss him?" The words were out before he could stop himself.

Putting her phone in the pocket of her jeans, she lifted her chin. "Nothing to do with you."

"I haven't slept since Tuesday night, I haven't eaten, I can't work—all because of you. So I'd say you promising kisses to all and sundry is very much my business."

"Well, welcome to the club. I haven't slept very much either, I haven't eaten, and I haven't been able to change the damn painting from a kiss to something else!"

He couldn't stop the grin. Stepping closer, he caught a whiff of her shampoo. His body immediately reacted. "Is that so?" he asked in a much softer voice.

Warily, she looked up at him. "We can't do this, Gavin. My life's a mess, and constantly thinking about you makes it worse!" She gestured wildly toward the several boxes in the room. "Look around you! And on top of everything, freaking Bill Norton refuses to send my paintings to the gallery in Livingston."

It was the slight quiver of her lower lip that made him forget all his previous resolve not to touch her again. He pulled her close, his hands stroking her back. For a long time, they stood like that, until she stopped shaking.

"You're constantly thinking about me?" He couldn't help smiling.

"It's not funny," she murmured against his chest.

"What about a nice cup of tea?"

When she looked up, her eyes were wet with tears, and groaning, he pulled her close again. "What happened? And who is Bill what's-his-name, and who the hell is the idiot you want to kiss?"

Sniffing, she pulled out of his arms. "Tea sounds like a

very good idea." He followed her as she walked toward the kitchen.

"Please sit down." She put on the kettle and took down cups from the cupboard.

He enjoyed watching her. She moved gracefully, purposefully. Underneath her eyes were dark circles, a clear indication she she'd been telling the truth about not sleeping, either.

When the water boiled, she made the tea. "Don't look at me—I'm a mess," she said, her eyes on the task at hand.

"You're beautiful. Always beautiful."

She looked up, the hot tea missed the cup and spilled on to the table "Oh, damn, look what you made me do!" In her effort to put the pot down, her hand landed in the hot beverage. "Ouch!"

He was next to her before she'd finished crying out. "Oh, babe," he crooned. Pulling her toward the sink, he opened the cold water and put her red fingers under the running water.

A tear escaped and ran down her cheek. He bent down and caught it with his lips as he closed the tap behind him.

Her breath hitched in her throat. "Gavin…"

But he didn't want to talk or think, his mouth closing over hers. Finally. Her scent surrounded him, seeped through every pore of his body until she was all he was aware of. This was why he was here. To be with her. Like this.

Soft arms slipped around his neck, and his tongue found its way to her welcoming, warm depths where it happily tangled with hers. He'd missed this. Missed her. Missed touching her, kissing her.

Angling his head, he deepened the kiss, but she suddenly pulled away, panting. "I'm already not thinking straight; you kissing me is not helping." And pulling out a chair, she quickly sat down.

He was out of breath, as well, his body ready for her. Inhaling deeply, he tried to get oxygen into his lungs.

Slowly, he sat down. "I want you—there's nothing phony about that."

She covered her face with her hands. "Don't say things like that!" Dropping her hands, she glared at him. "This whole fake-relationship thing is getting a life of its own, and I really don't need more difficulties in my life."

He finished pouring the tea before he spoke again. "What's going on? Can I help in any way?"

She shook her head, rubbing her temple. "Thank you, but I'll sort out my own messes."

"At least tell me what's going on?"

"It's no biggie. Up until now, a gallery in Missoula has curated my paintings, but the new manager, Bill Norton is…" She rubbed her arms. "To be honest, he gives me the creeps, and I've decided to move my paintings to another gallery in Livingston. What should have been an easy transition is turning out to be a problematic one. That's why I've phoned Guy, our family attorney. He'll try to sort it out. As I've said, I can handle my own problems."

"How old is this attorney?"

"Why is that important?"

"You've promised him a kiss."

The corners of her mouth lifted slightly. "I have, haven't I?"

"Brooke, damn it…"

"He's a friend of my mother's. Old enough to be my dad."

He exhaled audibly. "Good to know. So, is there anything I can do to help?" He already knew what her answer would be, but he had to try.

She shook her head. "No, thank you."

"What about if I help you with the packing?"

She shook her head. "Thanks, but you really don't have to. I can do this…"

"I know. You're a strong woman—raising a kid on your own, making a huge success of your passion, but let me help with something as mundane as packing up."

"It's not something you volunteer for if you don't have to."

"What if I want to?" he asked as he stood up.

"Why would you want to do that?"

He walked over to where she was sitting and bent down to kiss her. "Because you need help at the moment, and we're supposed to be a couple. Besides, that way I can be near you. And I like that. I can look at you, I can touch you and maybe even steal a kiss. And bonus"—he grinned before she could say anything—"I'll cook."

For the first time since he'd arrived, her eyes lit up. "Now that's an offer I can't refuse."

And then he simply had to kiss her again. "See, my first kiss."

The front door opened. "Mo-om!" Connor yelled. "I'm home. Is Uncle Gavin here? Is he going to cook?" He raced into the kitchen. "I'm hungry."

Brooke got up, her breath not quite steady yet, and bent down to hug her son. "You're always hungry."

"Let me make you a sandwich," Gavin said, smiling down at Connor. "And then you and I can go shop for food while your mom works a bit. What do you say?"

"Food! Yeah! I'm so, so hungry."

Gavin looked at Brooke. "So am I."

She covered her red cheeks with her hands. "I'm going upstairs."

Gavin caught her hand. "I've missed you," he whispered before his lips found hers.

"Ew!" Connor called out. "Do you have to do that?"

"I'm afraid so." Gavin grinned. "I really, really like her, you see."

But Connor had already forgotten about the kiss. He opened the fridge. "My sandwich?"

Gavin chuckled, turning to watch Brooke walk away. How priorities changed as one grew older. Food was the last thing on his mind at the moment.

CHAPTER 6

Brooke glanced warily at Gavin. He was putting the box he'd just closed next to the others in the hallway. After dinner, he'd helped her put Connor in bed and had then insisted on helping with packing up everything in the living and dining room.

The sexual tension in the room had been rising steadily over the last few hours. She put her hands on her back and stretched, trying to loosen up her sore muscles. "I think we're done here. Thank you so much for your help and especially for the lovely dinner. You're spoiling us."

Gavin grinned. "You're easy to spoil. What about the kitchen? Have you—?"

She shook her head adamantly. He had to leave and quickly, "Thank you, I'll manage. But thanks for helping out today."

He picked up his car keys. "It's easier when we lean on each other."

"I'm fine—you've done your share today, thanks."

H shrugged and moved toward to leave. "Okay, I'll pick up Connor on Saturday."

Brooke swallowed and opened the front door. He was just going to leave? Of course, he was leaving; that was what she wanted. Wasn't it?

His eyes were dark blue pools filled with messages she was too scared to decipher. "Goodnight, Brooke."

She focused on her hand . "Goodnight, Gavin."

He walked out, and she quickly closed the door. Her heart hammering away, she leaned against the door, listening for his footsteps. But she couldn't hear anything. Slowly, she opened the door again. He was still standing on the porch.

For long moments, they stared at each other.

"I want you. You have no idea how badly." His voice was barely a whisper.

"We can't. But maybe just a ki—"

She was in his arms, his mouth devouring hers before she'd finished speaking. He swung her inside the house, kicked the door shut without taking his mouth from hers.

His hands roamed restlessly over her back, kneading and caressing until her whole body was on fire. His scent surrounded her, sending her senses into overdrive. She leaned into the kiss, reveling in the feel of his stubble against her cheek, the warmth of his body under her fingers, his ragged breathing.

One of those clever hands closed around her breast. She nearly came undone right there and then. What he could do with those hands. Clinging to him, she tried to stay upright.

He lifted his head, gulping in air. "Damn, Brooke, you're killing me." He opened his mouth, closed it again, and when she blinked, he was gone, the front door closing behind him again.

She couldn't move. Her legs were too weak. With a laugh and a sob, she slid down to the floor and dropped her head on her knees. Oh. My.

Kissing and making love to her husband Adam had been a slow, relaxing, enjoyable experience. Kissing Gavin, though, was something entirely else. Looking down at her bare feet, she laughed on a sob. Her toes were happily curled inward.

He literally lit a fire inside her when their mouths met. Red-hot passion, the likes of which she'd never experienced before, threatened to devour her every time she was in his arms. Look at her—she was hot all over, her body shivering in anticipation, her breasts aching for his touch, her toes curling, for goodness' sake.

She hadn't known anyone could want another human being this much. She hadn't known passion could burn so brightly, so feverishly. And what she was feeling wasn't merely lust, it was so much more. If she wasn't cautious, she could easily lose her heart to this big South African. Something that could never happen. Besides the fact he was quite clear about not being interested in anything more than two weeks, she never wanted to give up control of her life again, like she'd done when she'd been married to Adam.

She'd blithely let him be in charge of their lives while she'd lost herself in her work. The feeling of complete and utter helplessness and panic, after his sudden demise, wasn't something she'd ever wanted to experience again.

Like her mother, she was what Logan called a free spirit. She would forget about time while she was painting; mundane things like eating and sleeping didn't matter all what much. Adam had made it easy for her to concentrate only on her work. But when he was gone, she quickly had to face reality. She had a little boy who needed her to be present and in charge.

A week ago, she still would've told anyone who'd have asked that she was actually managing her life quite well, thank you very much. Okay, she was forever looking for her phone and car keys, but at least she always knew where her son was. Except for the time he'd fetched Gavin to cook, of course.

And okay, she couldn't cook, but she remembered Connor had to eat and he kept her grounded. It would be irresponsible of her to allow someone to disrupt their lives for two weeks even if he kissed her senseless.

Her phone bleeped. It was a message. From Gavin.

A cold shower is supposed to help. It doesn't.

Her heart leapt. Her fingers were typing before she had time to think about what she was going to say.

I still can't move.

Three dots appeared. And were gone. The next minute her phone was ringing. It was a video call. From Gavin. Her heart went ballistic. With an unsteady hand, she clicked on the button. Gavin filled her whole screen. He wasn't wearing a shirt, his glorious, sexy six-pack on display on her phone. Right in front of her eyes. Oh. My.

"You're sitting on the floor," he said.

"I'm sitting on the floor."

"Why?"

"Seemed like a good idea at the time."

"Why?"

"My legs wouldn't carry me."

"Why?"

"Because you kissed me."

A slow smile appeared. "Is that so?"

She groaned out loud. "Gavin...you are...you make me feel things...Oh, damn, I can't believe I told you that! You're making me crazy!"

"There is a very obvious solution to our problem."

"What?"

"Let's have sex. It's clear, at this point, your rules and so-called contract are not going to keep us apart. We're way beyond 'just kissing,' babe, and you know it. I can't keep my hands off of you, if you hadn't noticed. I was thinking..."

"I don't like the sound of that..."

But he ignored her. "Everyone thinks we're a couple anyway, so it won't be strange if I sleep at your place until you move to the ranch. It's Thursday today; that means we'll have eight nights until next Friday. I know you have to work and I know Connor is around, but we'll have the nights to well, scratch the itch. When I leave for Seattle next Sunday, we'll tell everyone things didn't work out. By the time I get back, we'll just be friends again."

Just friends. How was she supposed to be "just friends" with Gavin after they'd made love? Made love. Where did that come from? He was proposing sex; nobody was talking about love. He wanted to scratch an itch, to be precise.

"Babe?"

"Let me get this straight—you're proposing an eight-night stand?"

"With a friend, I'd add."

"Eight-night stand with a friend to…what again? You've put it so eloquently? Oh, yes, to scratch an itch. Tempting, but I'll pass." Finally, she could feel her legs again, and she jumped up. "Goodnight, Gavin. I'll make sure Connor is ready for you on Saturday."

Bewildered, Gavin stared at the black screen on his phone. Well, hell. He'd thought by now he'd be on his way back to Brooke's place. She'd been going along with him for a while, he was sure of it, but then… Groaning out loud, he dropped his phone. He'd messed up the whole thing by calling having sex with her "scratching an itch."

What had happened to all his smooth moves? With Brooke…she scrambled his usual, logical thoughts, she shook him up, and to be honest, she scared him to death.

He walked to the window and stared out at the street. It was already dark outside, a crescent moon lying on its back his only companion. Rubbing his chest, he turned away and left his room. There was no way he was going to spend another night tossing and turning in bed. He had to start prepping for the first client he was going to see in Seattle; he might as well work.

Half an hour later, even though his laptop was open, he caught himself staring into space, thinking about Brooke, about Connor, about life on the ranch, about a damn German shepherd dog for the boy. What the hell was wrong with him?

Maybe it was time to be honest, with himself, at least. Brooke excited him, she awakened emotions and feelings he'd never experienced before, and because of her, he was dreaming about things he hadn't allowed himself to dream about before.

But, as he'd told her, he had nothing to offer her she didn't already have. She kept insisting she was quite capable of handling her own life, and she was right. As he knew all too well, he wasn't anybody's hero. He'd probably hurt her tonight, another reason why he should play his part in this charade without touching her again. And kissing her, even one more time, was definitely out of the question.

By the time Connor left for school Friday morning, Brooke had a splitting headache. Her phone rang as she waved him goodbye. It was Guy, the attorney. Her heart sank. The fact that he was calling only meant one thing—there was trouble.

"Hi, Guy," she greeted him, crossing her fingers.

"Brooke. We have a problem. I can take this further but…"

With a heavy heart she listened to Guy. Bill Norton had replied to Guy's email, insisting he'd only hand the paintings to Brooke and to her alone. Guy couldn't get hold of Lynda, either. He could take Bill to court, but that would take time and money; it might be quicker and less messy if she were to fetch the paintings herself.

"Okay, thanks, Guy. Let me get back to you. I appreciate your help. Do let me know what I owe you."

"Absolutely nothing. I'll do anything for Eleanor. You know I adore your mom." He chuckled before he ended the call.

Adored her mother? That was interesting. She'd never thought of her mom with anyone else. She had to remember to ask her mom about him.

She sank down on the nearest chair. After another sleepless night dreaming steamy dreams about the very sexy Gavin Wilson, she was in no mood to deal with anyone, let alone Bill Norton, but Guy was right. If she wanted this over soon, she should drive to Missoula and get her paintings. A long, drawn-out court case was not something she even considered. She simply didn't have the time or the emotional capacity at this point.

Checking her watch, she dialed her mother's number. Her head was buzzing. It was about a three-hour drive. If nothing unforeseen happened, she could be back in Alisson later tonight.

"Brooke, darling, I'm so glad you called. I've found you the most beautiful wedding dress—"

Brooke groaned out loud. "Mom, seriously, I don't have time for this now. Please listen…" She quickly explained she was on her way to Missoula and asked her mom to pick up Connor after school.

"I should be back tonight. I'll fetch him tomorrow… Oh, I just remembered. Gavin was going to pick him up tomorrow—"

"Don't you worry about that, my dear girl, just go. I'll text Gavin. And if it's too late tonight, please rather stay over in Missoula or even Butte but don't drive in the dark."

"Okay, thanks, Mom. By the way, Guy doesn't want any payment from me; he says he adores you."

It was quiet for such a long time, Brooke checked her phone to see whether her mom was still on the line. She was. "Mom?"

"Well, really," her mom finally said. "He's never told me that. Okay, off you go—and don't worry about Connor!"

The line was dead before Brooke could ask another

question. There had been something in her mom's voice...
Smiling, Brooke sprinted up the stairs. Her mom liked
meddling in everyone else's lives; maybe Brooke should
return the favor at some point.

But that would have to wait until she got back from
Missoula.

CHAPTER 7

Gavin had just settled in front of his computer with a steamy cup of coffee Friday morning when his phone bleeped. His heart leapt, but it wasn't Brooke, it was her mother.

Brooke is on her way to Missoula. Connor staying with us.

He read the message again. Brooke was on her way to Missoula? Why? What had she said about Missoula? She had paintings there—the guy gave her the creeps…

Cussing, he jumped up, grabbed his car keys and sunglasses, and raced out of the house. The damn woman. Of course, she wouldn't ask: she could do everything on her own, even facing a creepy guy. But hell, there was no way he was letting her drive alone to Missoula to deal with someone who gave her the creeps.

Within seconds, he was behind the wheel of his car and was driving down the street. Inhaling deeply, he tried to calm down. Telling Brooke Johnson he wasn't "letting" her drive to Missoula would be so the wrong thing to say. By this time, he knew her well. He'd have to find another way to persuade her to let him accompany her.

She was pulling out of her driveway just as he was approaching her house. He stepped on the gas and parked behind her. Her car shuddered to a halt, and the next minute, her door flew open. She was livid. And absolutely gorgeous, although perhaps telling her that at this precise moment would also probably be the wrong move. In a short, frilly-kinda skirt and a top with tiny buttons from top to bottom, she took his breath away. His fingers twitched. Those buttons…

A livid Brooke, he could handle. It was the idea that anyone would hurt her that freaked him out.

"What are you doing here?" Brooke demanded, hands on hips.

He rolled down the car window and slipped his sunglasses down slightly. "Heard you have to get to Missoula. It so happens I'm on my way there, as well. Hop in. My SUV has more space. In case you need it."

Her eyes narrowed; her mouth opened and closed a few times. "I can do this on my own…"

"I know. I could get into your car if you'd rather drive, but it would be silly not to share a ride when both of us are going to the same place at the same time, don't you think?"

She crossed her arms. "Why do you have to go to Missoula?"

"I have to see someone. And you?"

She glared at him. "I also have to see someone."

"So, hop in and we can go and see the someones we need to see." He looked at his watch. "It's half-past eight; we should be there at around eleven. Depending on how long it takes you to see your someone, we should be back by nightfall."

She stared at him for a moment longer. He swore he could hear her mind working. Finally, she threw her hand in the air. "Okay, but so you know—no touching and no kissing are allowed. Let me get my bag."

It was an effort, but he managed a straight face. "Yes, ma'am."

With another suspicious glare in his direction, she

stomped back to her car. Grinning, he took out his phone and sent Eleanor a quick text.

Gavin had turned on the radio, and soothing blues sounds filled the car. Brooke leaned back and closed her eyes. Truth be told, she was very glad not to be driving to Missoula alone. And bonus, Gavin's SUV was actually big enough so that she could bring the two paintings back herself. She'd planned on having them shipped to Livingston, but now it wouldn't be necessary.

Normally, she loved driving, but she hadn't slept much since…well, since this guy had kissed her silly on Monday night. She hadn't had so many erotic, steamy dreams at night since…well, never.

A mere four days ago. Since then, she'd suddenly become aware of her own needs again. Over the past three years, there simply hadn't been time to think about kissing, much less having sex. Since Monday though, she'd rediscovered the wonder of being touched, of being kissed by someone who knew how, and who seemed to be so tuned into what she wanted, he knew exactly what turned her on.

But it's not real—something she had a hard time remembering. It was fake and it was temporary; he had been very clear about that. It would be so easy to reach out and touch his hand. He would hold her hand tightly, like he always did, and he would smile at her. She liked the light in his eyes, as if the smile was just for her.

Oh, damn, there she was, dreaming about the impossible again. Was his six-pack really as rock-hard as it had looked on her phone last night? She'd love to glide her hands all over those muscles, to feel the heat of his naked flesh underneath…

Her breath hitched in her throat, and she quickly sat upright.

"Everything okay?" Gavin asked.

She shook her head. "Not really."

"Anything I can do to help?"

She opened her mouth to answer him, but he cut off her words with a short laugh.

"You don't need me, I know. There isn't anything I can do for you, and you don't need or want anything from me. Got it."

He wasn't angry, just resigned.

With a sigh, she turned toward him. "It's not that I don't need you, it's just...I have a thing about not letting anyone else take over my life again. Adam and I married straight out of college. It was about the same time there was interest in my work. So, he took care of everything and left me to blithely paint and ignore the rest of the world. After he was gone..." She shook her head. "Trying to figure out what was going on was so overwhelming, and if I didn't have Logan and my mom's attorney friend, it would've taken me much longer to know about my own affairs. I promised myself I'll never be in such a position again. I have to know what's going on, I have to make my own decisions, and I have to sort out my own messes."

Gavin was quiet for a while before he spoke again. "Did Adam take care of Connor, as well?"

"Well, no. He was at work during the day but when he was home, he'd helped."

"In other words, you took care of Connor even while you were earning money with your paintings?"

She nodded. "Yes, but..."

"No buts. From where I'm sitting, you did your part. My dad used to call my mom his 'partner'—that's how their marriage worked, he explained. Sounds to me you were a great partner."

She pressed her lips together. "Look at you handing out relationship advice. So how come you've never married?"

He grimaced. "Told you, I'm not marriage material."

"Why do you say that? Because of your last girlfriend?

74

What was her name?"

"Sarah. Yeah. She told me I'm not relationship material. She's right. I'm useless in the dating game. I tend to always screw things up."

"What happened with Sarah?"

"I found out she was cheating on me."

"She was cheating on you, and she thinks you're the one who's not relationship material? Surely you can see the irony in that? She's the one with the problem, not you."

"I couldn't make her happy."

"It's not your job to make anybody else happy! You're a great guy, Gavin, and any girl would be lucky to date you."

He grinned cheekily. "Yeah?"

She laughed. "Well, now that we've psychoanalyzed one another, why are you going to Missoula?"

"Told you. I'm going to see someone. Why are you going to Missoula?"

The penny finally dropped. "So someone told you I'm going to Missoula? My mother or one of your sisters?"

"Your mother."

"And let me guess. It was around the same time you suddenly had to see someone in Missoula, as well?"

"You could interpret it like that, yeah."

"Seriously, Gavin, I told you…"

Glancing in her direction, he took her hand. "I know. But I've told you, we can lean on each other. I hear that's how relationships work."

"This is not a relationship."

"Let's see: I've kissed you, I've touched you, you've kissed me back, you've put your hands on me. And I'm going with you to Missoula. I'd call it a relationship."

"A fake relationship, remember? And anyway, it's not as if we're going on a dirty weekend together…" Oh, no, had she really said that out loud? "I mean…"

He was shaking with laughter.

"It's not funny!" she cried out. "When I'm around you,

I say and do things…" Groaning, she rubbed her face. She shouldn't have said that. What was wrong with her, seriously?

He picked up her hand and kissed it. "Babe, I can't think of anything I'd rather do than going away on a dirty weekend with you."

"I'm just saying none of this is real. We're pretending to like each other, to…to be a couple, to get our families to stop pestering us. Remember that."

With his eyes on the road, he opened her hand and planted a hot, wet kiss right in the middle of her palm. She felt his lips all the down to her very core. "Gavin…" Was that sultry, husky voice really hers?

"How does that make you feel?" he asked.

"That's not the point," she mumbled.

"How does that make you feel?"

"What do you think?"

"Too chicken, huh? Can I…may I…tell you what I feel?" He glanced at her before he looked back at the road.

"You may." Oh, my goodness, listen to her—she sounded like a prim schoolteacher.

He kissed her hand again. "I want you."

"That's not a feeling!"

"Of course it's a feeling."

"No, telling me what you feel would be you saying something like, 'you make me happy' or 'you make my dopamine levels go all silly' or even something like, 'I'll break my rules for you' or 'you're all my heart ever talks about'—you can't just say 'I want you.'"

The next moment, he stepped on the brakes and pulled off the road.

"What are you do—"

But his mouth was on hers, hot and urgent, before she could finish her sentence. Within seconds, she was clinging to him, scared to death he'd stop kissing her.

His one hand cradled her head while the other roamed freely over her shoulders, down her arms, up her sides until those clever fingers folded over an aching breast.

He lifted his head. "I have to see you, babe," he pleaded.

With her eyes on him, she slowly slid open the top button of her blouse. His gaze followed her every move, his ragged breathing filling the space of the inside of his SUV. When she slid open the third button, he pushed her hands out of the way and opened the rest himself.

For long moments, he stared into her eyes before he looked down. "I don't talk about my feelings and I don't have fancy words for you, but I've never wanted anyone the way I want you right now." His gravelly voice sent delicious shivers down her spine. "A red bra. Damn, babe, I'm already rock-hard for you, I don't know…"

With a groan, he slipped a hand into the one cup. Finally, flesh on flesh, skin on skin. She was burning up. Her head fell back. "Gavin…"

"Tell me what you feel?"

"You make me hot, so hot…" she murmured.

He dropped his hand, and her eyes flew open. "What…?"

His hands were back on the steering wheel, his teeth clenched together, the muscle in his cheek jumping up and down. With a backward glance, he started the car again and slipped onto the road. "The first time I make love to you will be in a bed, not a damn car."

With unsteady hands, she tried to button her top up again, but it was a struggle. They were both breathing heavily and her gaze kept straying to the very clear indication of his desire.

The giggle came out of nowhere, but once she'd started, she couldn't stop.

"What so damn funny?" he growled.

"We are. I'm thirty-three and I'm making out in a car. On the highway. In the middle of a Thursday morning! Who does that?"

With a satisfied grin, he took her hand in his again.

"Two people who obviously can't keep their hands off of each other. And I have just one thing to say about feelings. I want you."

That quickly sobered her up. But what happened to these feelings when he left for Seattle? Would it be as easy to bury what she felt as it was to switch off a light? And what would she do if it didn't work? Her body was burning for his touch, and she had an idea that it wasn't something that was going to change soon.

So much for no touching and no kissing.

CHAPTER 8

It was just after twelve when Gavin parked his SUV in a parking garage in downtown Missoula. He'd never been here before, but Brooke obviously knew her way around and could direct him. They'd made two stops along the way. She'd been silent since the last one.

"Missoula is a beautiful city," he said conversationally as they got out of the car. "Surrounded by mountains, forests, and the views I've seen of the river that runs through it, it's something else."

She smiled, although she was fidgeting, a sign, he knew by now, she was apprehensive. "The Clark Fork River. And the mountains are the Rockies, five different mountain ranges, I've read somewhere. Inhabitants like to tell you how deer pass through their front yards. Sometimes, you can see moose from the road, and I've heard even bears venture downtown to Greenough Park."

"Sounds like a great place to live."

"I agree. It's also a tourist favorite. Apart from the scenery, there is a variety of choices for the culturally minded local or tourist. Whether it's art or music being created in the street, or a gala event at a local museum, Missoula has what it takes to satisfy even the most avant-garde individual."

Looking down at her, he smiled. Mmm, a perfect place to bring Brooke to for that dirty weekend she'd talked about. He sobered quickly. By next weekend, he'd be on his way to Seattle, and by the time he returned to Alisson, they would carry on as friends only.

"The person you have to see—are they close by?" he asked as they walked toward the elevator.

"Yes, quite close. There's a diner nearby where you can meet me once you've seen your...person." And with a knowing smile, she stepped into the elevator.

She clearly suspected he wasn't really seeing anyone, but she wasn't asking any more questions.

She pressed a button, and the elevator moved. They were alone, and shifting to stand behind her, he put his hands on her shoulders. Her muscles were tense, confirming how on edge she actually was. He dug his thumbs into her hard muscles, and a low groan escaped her lips.

"You're so tense," he said. "Anything to do with the person you're about to see?"

"I'm fine. It's probably from standing in front of an easel most of my days."

"I can come with you if you want me to? All you have to do is ask."

"I told you I can handle my own mess."

So there was a mess to be handled, but of course, she wasn't about to tell him. She was really sticking to her guns about managing her own life, even if she was clearly dreading meeting whoever she was about to see.

The elevator stopped. He took her hand as they walked out of the building.

She pointed to her right. "Over there is the diner I spoke about. I don't know how long your meeting will be," she said with a slight emphasis on *your*, "but I shouldn't be longer than half an hour."

He pulled her closer and kissed her. Her mouth was

shivering slightly. "Babe, you okay?"

She pulled her handbag closer to her. "Of course. I'm not used to someone kissing me in the middle of a busy street. See you later!" With a wave of her hand, she walked in the opposite direction of where the diner is.

He waited until she'd disappeared around the corner before he followed her.

By the time Brooke entered the gallery, she was clutching her bag tightly, holding on for dear life. She was more nervous than she'd cared to admit, even to herself. Maybe she should've asked Gavin to come with her; she was not looking forward to confronting Bill Norton. She hadn't even let him know she was coming; he might not be here.

A quick glance around the gallery made it clear her paintings had been taken down. She walked farther into the big room before she spotted Bill. So he was here.

He'd been talking to two clients but the moment he saw her, he excused himself and walked toward her with a big, creepy smile. "Brooke, darling. What a lovely surprise. I—"

"I'm here to get my paintings, Bill. If you'd given them to the people I've arranged to pick them up, I wouldn't have had to waste a whole day driving to Missoula. I've also emailed Lynda, so she'll learn about your behavior as soon as she's able to read her mails."

His creepy smile didn't waver. "Why so hostile? Getting an attorney to send me threatening letters—it is all so unnecessary! Lynda is on her cruise; we don't have to bother her with this. I just wanted to see your lovely face again. I told you I like to have a more…intimate relationship with my artists."

"I am not 'your' anything. My paintings, please?" She didn't want to make a scene, but if that was what it was going to take to reach her goal, she had no qualms doing so.

"Of course, darling," he said and put a hand on her shoulder. "I just have a form you need to sign. You do realize I couldn't just hand over your paintings to anyone?"

She shrugged off his arm and glared at him. "Don't touch me. Where is the form?"

"In my office, of course." Bill reached out to touch her again, but she backed away quickly. From behind, two familiar hands folded protectively over her shoulders. "Everything okay, babe?" It was Gavin. He was here.

For a brief moment, she experienced relief—going with Bill to his office alone was not something she was looking forward to, but Gavin didn't have to know that. She would've handled whatever happened on her own. Hadn't she told him that?

She turned to face Gavin. "I've got this."

Gavin smiled, although it didn't quite reach his eyes. "Of course you have. I'm just here to help carry your paintings."

She'd already thought about what she'd do with the paintings, but she still hadn't come up with a workable solution. Gavin had just made it easy. The two paintings were big, but not that big; they should be able to carry them back. But she didn't have to like his interference. With another glare in the direction of both men, she squared her shoulders and marched toward Bill's office. "Let's get this over with. This is not acceptable and I'll make sure everyone knows about this little episode."

"I don't know what all the fuss is about." Bill smiled as they entered his office. "I told Brooke…"

He put out a tentative hand to touch her again, but she shrank back against Gavin.

Gavin put his arm around her. "The lady told you not to touch her."

"Who are you again?"

"Not someone you want to mess with. The paintings. Now." Gavin didn't even sound threatening; he simply towered over Bill.

"Of course." Bill scuttled away.

By the time they reached Gavin's car in the parking lot, Brooke was still shaking and breathing deeply. What a distasteful incident. She was definitely going to send Lynda another email to complain about the very unpleasant Bill. Chances were, she wasn't the only one Bill was trying to intimidate.

Gavin had still been glaring at Bill when she'd simply picked up one of her paintings and left the office. She hadn't looked back again but had heard Gavin's footsteps behind her as they'd left the gallery.

She put the painting down next to the car. It had been a while since she'd last had to carry one of her own paintings. Gulping in some air, she leaned against the door. She shouldn't be so out of breath after walking a few blocks. Hopefully, once she was on the ranch, she'd be able to get more exercise.

But then maybe her heavy breathing had nothing to do with carrying the painting and everything to do with the silent man next to her. Gavin hadn't said a word since they'd left the gallery.

"Gavin, I…"

That muscle in his cheek was working overtime. He didn't answer—just opened the door for her.

She squared her shoulders. "I would've been able to get the paintings on my own; nobody asked you to barge in and take over. Bill is creepy, but I don't believe he would've done anything…"

At this point, Gavin's eyes were mere slits, and with a cussword, he turned away. "Get in the damn car."

"I don't have to do…"

He rounded on her, eyes blazing, but she stood her ground. "I am not sure whether to throttle you or kiss you…" The next minute, he hauled her close to him and buried his face in her neck, a shudder wracking his body. "Do you have any idea how worried I was? Anything could've happened to you!"

"Gavin…" she tried, but he only tightened his hold on her.

She slid her hands up and down his shoulders, trying to soothe him. They stood like that for a long while before he finally stopped shaking and her insides settled down.

He kissed her hard before he cupped her face. "That damn man put a hand on you…" Inhaling, he stepped away and rubbed his face. "I'm here. Why the hell didn't you ask me to go with you?"

"Because it's my mess. I was going to sort it out."

"Damn it to hell, Brooke—you could've been hurt! That guy isn't just creepy, he was hell-bent on getting you in his office alone. There wasn't even a form to sign! Don't you think you're taking this I-can-do-it-on-my-own thing a tad too far?"

She swallowed. Gavin was right. Bill hadn't even mentioned the so-called "form" again. Brooke crossed her arms. "I have to be able to sort out my own life, damn it. I don't need you!"

Something flashed in his eyes. "Of course you don't." He turned and put the paintings away.

Brooke quickly got into the car. She was on the verge of bursting into tears. What she wanted to do was throw herself into Gavin's arms. She was aching for him to hold and comfort her. But she had to remember he was leaving next week.

For the first hour, Gavin drove in silence. He didn't trust himself to speak. Those few moments he'd noticed that man's hand on Brooke, he'd seen red. At the same time, he'd realized he couldn't punch the guy like every instinct in him was urging him to do.

He had two strong, independent sisters, and he'd

realized early on that Brooke might not always know where her phone was, but she'd been raising a little boy on her own while earning a living by working extremely hard. She also was another strong, independent woman, and if he'd learned anything from his sisters, it was not to take over or take charge of their lives, even though he'd always found it extremely difficult to just watch from the sidelines.

And when Lindsay had really needed him, he hadn't even noticed she'd been in trouble.

If Brooke had been hurt, or... Inhaling slowly, he tried to calm down. He should've insisted to go with her right from the start. This whole thing could've been avoided, if only she'd spoken to someone. Spoken to him.

He glanced in her direction. She'd closed her eyes, but her hands were still clutching the seat tightly. Leaning over toward her, his eyes on the road, he took her hand in his. Better. At least when he touched her, he knew she was okay.

She didn't open her eyes, but her hand slowly relaxed in his. Something shifted inside him. What the hell was he doing? He had no business interfering with Brooke's life. She was right. They'd be breaking up in a week's time.

After a few miles, they were nearing the neighboring town, Butte. Brooke opened her eyes and sat upright. She pulled her hand out of his and he let it go. No use hanging on to someone who didn't want him around; Sarah had taught him that lesson.

Brooke cleared her throat. "I'm sorry. You're right, I should've asked you to come with me. It's just...I can't let myself depend on you. This thing between us...it's not a permanent arrangement and when you're gone, I'll have to rely on myself again."

He opened his mouth to protest but closed it again. She was right. He didn't have anything to offer her, and she would've been able to handle the nasty little man all by herself, he had no doubt.

An unfamiliar hole opened up inside him, and he rubbed his chest. He should make sure to stay far away from the lovely widow until he left for Seattle.

CHAPTER 9

It was around eight o'clock when they drove back into Alisson. Brooke glanced quickly in Gavin's direction. He'd put down his sunglasses, but it was still difficult to judge his mood.

It had been a quiet trip back. After she'd pulled her hand out of his, Gavin hadn't touched her again and she felt...bereft. Which was ridiculous. They should end this whole charade sooner rather than later. Her poor heart wouldn't survive being this close to Gavin for much longer.

After Adam's untimely passing, she'd never really thought about dating again. She'd always put it off. Somewhere in the future, she figured, she'd find someone she could spend time with. What she'd never expected was the very strong attraction between her and Gavin, the desire that grabbed her by the throat whenever she was near him, the heat between them. And when he kissed her and held her, she felt like the most beautiful woman in the world.

She'd never before experienced any of the feelings she had around Gavin. She'd been married to a good man and she'd loved him, but this craziness, this burning passion was a first. Surely it wasn't something that could last: it was way too intense. There was Connor to consider. She couldn't just jump into the arms of the first man she lusted after.

Turning her head, she stared out of the window. Her body reacted to this man even when he wasn't touching her.

They'd finally reached the street where she lived. He slowed down and parked his car in front of her house.

"Do you need my help carrying the paintings?" he asked.

"Yes, thank you. If you could maybe just put them inside the house. I'll arrange for them to be shipped to the gallery in Livingston. Sally will be so happy." She was talking way too much, too nervously, and quickly got out of the car.

Gavin opened the door at the back of his SUV, and within moments, she was unlocking the front door. He put the painting inside, made a quick second trip, and immediately stepped out onto the porch again.

"Goodnight, Brooke."

"Gavin…"

He didn't look at her. "I'll try to stay out of your way until I leave for Seattle."

Stunned, she stared at him. "What about our fake relationship? It was your idea, remember?"

He grimaced. "I know. We'll let it play out until next week. I may leave earlier than planned." Finally, his gaze found hers, but just for a moment before he turned away. He looked tired. And there was something else she couldn't quite put her finger on.

Brooke was frozen to the spot. He was walking out of her life. He was going to leave next week anyway; maybe his idea of "scratching an itch" wasn't such a bad idea. There was at least a possibility that after they'd made love, these strange feelings between them would settle. Maybe they'd even be able to laugh about it at some point, much later on.

He'd reached his car.

"Gavin!" She wasn't quite sure why she was calling him, but she couldn't let him leave, not like this.

He ignored her and opened the door or his car. Her feet finally got wings, and she flew out of the house, down the steps, and reached his side of the car just as he sat down.

"Gavin..." She hadn't thought this through. "I mean..."

"What do you want, Brooke?" he asked, his eyes hooded.

And then it was so easy to say. "You. I want you." She held out her hand.

For long moments, he stared at her. "You sure?"

She nodded.

"I need to hear the words, babe."

"I want to be with you. I've never been more sure of anything before. And you have to know—what I feel when I'm with you, I've never felt before."

Before she could blink, she was in his arms, and he was carrying her toward the house. His teeth were clenched together, the muscle in his cheek jumping up and down. Fascinated, she stroked over it, loving the sensation of his stubble against her hand.

He tried to open the door with his elbow, but it refused to budge. Cursing softly, he put her down. In any other similar circumstances, she probably would've laughed, but there was nothing funny about the way her heart was racing at the moment. If she couldn't get her hands on him within the next few seconds, she was going to burst into flames.

He pushed the door open and helped her inside before he kicked it closed behind them. He stared at her. They were both breathing hard.

Slowly, he lifted his hand and touched her face. It was such a small gesture, but she felt his touch right down to her toes. Grabbing onto his shirt with both hands, she pulled him closer. And finally his mouth was on hers.

She slipped her arms around his body and held on. A current simply picked her up, and she gratefully capitulated. This was what she'd been craving for since...the first time she'd seen him, to be honest. To be this close to him, to feel the heat of his skin under her fingers, to inhale his scent, to kiss him like this.

She was soft and lean, satin and roses. Within seconds, her scent had penetrated his skin, become part of his blood, and was racing through his body. Her fingers pulled at his shirt; he quickly plucked it over his head.

"Your room?" He hardly recognized his own voice, laced with desire.

Her gaze was on her hands, which had lazily begun to explore his chest. "Up the stairs, first one to the right." It was just a murmur, but he'd heard her. He knew where her room was, she was not just giving him directions, she was giving him permission.

"You sure?"

She slipped her arms around his neck. "I'm sure."

That was all he needed to know. His body burning, he swung her up in his arms again and took the steps two at a time.

"Connor?" he asked as he glanced toward the boy's door.

"On the ranch, with Mom," she said with her lips against his throat.

He staggered across the hallway to her room. It wasn't quite dark outside yet; the room was filled with shadows. Gently, he put her down. For a millisecond, they stared at each other.

"You're all I can think about," he murmured as he pulled her close again. Her lips were hot, feverish against his, her hands unsteady as they moved restlessly over his shoulders. She pulled back, and with her eyes on him, she lifted her top over her head.

"I was looking forward to unbuttoning those again." He grinned but he sobered quickly.

Her hands had disappeared behind her back. With her gaze never leaving his, she unfastened her bra, slipped it down her arms, and let it drop.

Taking in every detail of her gorgeous face, he let his hand slide down her body, down between the contours of her breasts, until he reached the top of her jeans. "You're so, so beautiful." And with a groan, he claimed her lips again.

They'd somehow ended up on the bed, but she was only vaguely aware of her surroundings. Those hands. Caressing her breasts, teasing, tempting, demanding, tormenting. She was burning up, her heart hammering away.

"Finally," he crooned before his mouth closed around an aching nipple. She nearly came undone right there. She wrapped his hair around her fingers, urging him on, keeping him in place, dreading the moment he would stop.

His hands slid farther down her body, lighting fires right below the surface of her skin. When he reached the fastening of her jeans, a soft curse slipped out.

Giggling, she quickly lifted her body from the bed, and with his help, they shoved her jeans all the way down. He threw them to the side, his eyes raking her from head to toe. All she was remained wearing was a very small, red triangle.

"You're killing me, you know that?" Standing up, he loosened his belt.

It was her turn to enjoy the show. Leaning back on her elbows, she slid her gaze over him. He had a beautiful body—all hard lines and muscles. Slowly, he pushed down his jeans. Her eyes widened. No briefs and…wow.

"Like what you see?" he asked cheekily as he knelt beside her.

"I do," she breathed, putting out a hand to touch him. "No briefs?"

"Hate the things…" With a groan, he caught her wandering hand. "If you touch me, this will be over way too soon. I want more of you." Stretching out next to her, he pulled her closer. "I haven't even begun…to…"

"Yeah?"

"Oh, yeah."

His mouth found hers again while his hands were now free to journey over her body without any hindrance. Or, wait… He lifted his head. She was still wearing the small, red triangle. With his gaze on hers, he slipped his hand under the elastic.

Her breath hitched, her eyes darkening as her body arched upward. Leisurely moving his hand farther down, he kept his gaze on her.

"Gavin…" she whispered, her body moving restlessly.

"What do you want?" Slowly, he moved his fingers closer and closer toward her heat. It was taking all his control not to rush her.

She moaned, moving her head from side to side.

"Tell me?" he insisted.

"Touch me," she pleaded.

That was all he'd been waiting for. He tried to shove down the lace and satin, but for something so tiny, it wouldn't budge.

"Let me…" she began, but he was done waiting. He ripped the small piece from her body, his fingers finally finding her heat.

With a cry, her body arching up, he watched her reaching the first peak. As she slowly opened her eyes, he pulled her closer. "Again."

She'd reached and crested that pinnacle so many times, but Gavin wouldn't let her catch her breath. His hands were all over her, taking her to heights she'd never experienced before.

Outside, the sun had set, people were going about their evening rituals, unwinding after a long day. A car honked. In the distance, a child laughed. But she was only vaguely aware of life outside the cocoon she and Gavin were in.

Their bodies were slick from the heat. Desire was a living, breathing creature, egging her on to give him as much pleasure as she possibly could. Throwing her leg over him, she pushed him back against the pillows. "My turn." And with her gaze on his, her mouth trailed a path over his hot flesh. But just as she reached her goal, he lifted himself and flipped her over so that she was again lying beneath him.

Panting, he grabbed something from his pants. Protection. She hadn't even thought about that. Gulping, she tried to get much-needed oxygen into her lungs before she helped him, reveling in the feel of his throbbing desire in her hand.

With a laugh, he moved her hand aside and lifted himself above her. "I want to be inside you."

He wanted to watch her crest one more time, but the moment her silky heat closed around him, he knew he wasn't going to last much longer. He began to move. She grabbed onto his shoulders, and together they quickly found their rhythm. They stayed in sync, every step of the way, as if they'd been doing this for a long time.

He tried to keep his eyes on her, but a red haze of desire shifted in front of him, making it impossible to focus. His head fell backward, and with her name a mantra on his lips, this time he reached the pinnacle with her.

Brooke slowly opened her eyes. The sun was up, birds were singing. Slowly she turned her head. She was alone in her bed. Of course, she was alone. Why would Gavin stay?

Lifting the sheet, she peeked at herself. Groaning, she quickly pulled it back up. She was buck naked. And she'd spent a whole night like that with Gavin.

Images of their entwined bodies flashed before her eyes. Groaning out loud, she dropped her face in her hands. If she lived to be a hundred, she'd never forget last night. Making love with Gavin was extraordinary. It had been their first time together, but he'd known exactly what she'd wanted, as if they'd been together numerous times before.

Connor. Her mother. Quickly she sat up and grabbed her phone, clutching the sheet against her body.

Her mother answered immediately. "Brooke! So lovely to hear from you. Did you get your paintings back?"

"Yes, thanks, Mom. I…I've slept in. I'll come fetch Connor as soon as I'm dressed."

"Why don't you let him stay a bit longer? He's outside with Logan. The dogs are following him around, like they do when's he's here. Come this afternoon, and we'll all have dinner together."

"Uhm…okay, thanks, Mom. I'll see you later." She put the phone down and let her eyes close, let her head fill with indulgent images from the night before.

"Everything okay?"

Startled, she turned toward the door. Gavin was entering the room, tray in hand, no shirt. The top button of his jeans was left open. Her mouth literally watered as he slowly approached the bed.

"I…I thought you'd left," she stammered.

Grinning, he put the tray down and settled down next to her on the mattress. "Not while there is a beautiful woman lying naked in the bed."

Oh, so he was making jokes while she was all hot and

bothered? She dropped the sheet. His smile disappeared, and he inhaled sharply.

"Babe…" Two big hands covered her breasts. "These…are the holy grail," he whispered as he lowered his head.

Her eyes closed. And she knew. She loved this man with an intensity that left her reeling. A sharp sword went straight through her heart.

Temporary. It's temporary. And it wasn't real. A fake relationship. Although there was nothing fake about what this man made her feel.

Slipping her arms around his shoulders, she held on tightly. When they left the house in a few hours, everything that had happened between them would stay behind, right here.

After next week, Gavin would be gone, and she'd have to carry on with her and Connor's lives without his cooking, without his help, and especially without his lovemaking.

Without him.

CHAPTER 10

The trip to the ranch was silent. Gavin had Brooke's hand in his, his teeth clenched tightly together. There was a hole inside of him the size of the wide, open spaces of the Karoo back in South Africa, and his heart seemed to hover somewhere outside of his body.

He probably should've said something during the night, but he hadn't wanted to waste any time yapping when he could've been making love to her. They'd hardly slept. Each time she'd turned or he'd moved, they'd ended up touching one another, and each touch ignited the embers of desire that had never quite died during the long, dark hours. He simply couldn't get enough of her—not something that would change anytime soon. In the end, she had to send him out of her room that morning so she could get dressed; otherwise they'd probably still be in her shower.

Since they'd left her house, she'd become quiet.

He didn't want whatever it was between him and Brooke to end, but he was leaving for Seattle next week, she had work to do. Life continued even if he wanted to hold on to every minute he could spend with her. He didn't have anything to offer her she didn't already have, he knew that, but maybe they could be together for a little while longer.

Taking the turn-off to the ranch, he glanced at her. "I can stay with you for the rest of the week."

Her head whipped in his direction. "So, we're back to the eight-night stand? Or how long would it be now? Seven days? Six?"

Before he could open his mouth, though, she continued, "I don't want to confuse Connor. He likes you a lot. It'll break his heart if he thinks you're staying and then you up and disappear after a day or two when you have to leave for Seattle."

"I was hoping after last night you might have changed your mind." He parked in front of Eleanor's home on the ranch.

"Last night we scratched the itch. If I remember correctly, that was exactly what you proposed."

He grabbed her hand. "It was way more than scratching an itch, and you know it!"

She didn't look at him—only smiled vaguely in his direction. "Do I?" Before he could react, she'd opened her door.

Connor was already racing toward his mom with Eleanor a little bit behind him.

"Mom! Gavin!" He threw his arms around his mother before he ran toward Gavin. "I've been waiting and waiting for you. Come on, I want to show you the horses."

Gavin looked down at the little boy with his mom's beautiful blue eyes. He smiled. "Let me say hi to your grandma, and then I'm all yours."

"Eleanor." He nodded and bent down to give her a hug.

Eleanor's eyes narrowed slightly before they moved between him and Brooke. "Something happened...?"

But Brooke grabbed her mother's arm. "Come on, Mom, let's go to Lindsay. I want to see the baby's room before I go and check how my house is doing." And with a wave, the two women started down the short path toward the house where Lindsay and Blake lived.

With a last glance at the gorgeous woman who'd managed to turn his world upside down within a week, Gavin took Connor's hand. "Lead away. I can't wait to see the horses."

His thoughts chaotic, he tried to listen to what Connor was saying, but he kept looking back over his shoulder, and the hole inside of him got bigger.

He should leave for Seattle sooner, rather than later. What he'd experienced with Brooke last night had been so much more than merely scratching an itch, but she obviously didn't feel the same way. Maybe he would stop thinking about her all the time when he was in another state, another city.

By late afternoon, the men were barbequing outside. Brooke was in the kitchen with Charlie and Lindsay, making a salad.

She'd been aware of the way Gavin's two sisters and her mother had been watching her and Gavin all afternoon. Hopefully, they wouldn't say anything because she was afraid she might just burst into tears if anyone were to ask about yesterday.

Last night had been magical, extraordinary. She'd never been good with words, but she knew she'd be able to express with her brushes and oils how deeply she loved Gavin, how intensely she wanted him. In her mind's eye, images, shapes, and colors were already forming, pressing her to pick up her brushes.

She needed him, not just to find her phone or to step in when she was struggling, but because he somehow got her, accepted all her foibles in his stride. Even the fact that she couldn't cook didn't seem to bother him at all.

And she'd also discovered he was the only man who'd ever be able to bring her the kind of pleasure she'd experienced last night. He'd taken her to heights she'd never experienced before.

No wonder she'd been painting kissing him, way before she'd even known how she felt about him. She'd loved him all along. Probably since the day she'd met him. Her heart had known long before her brain had caught on.

What still blew her mind was that they'd been so in tune with one another: her body had instinctively known how to respond to his every touch, while her hands had been strangely familiar with every nook and cranny of his muscled body. Her intuition showed her what he'd wanted, what he'd needed.

Making love with Gavin had been a life-changing experience.

And his only take from the night? *I can stay with you for the rest of the week.*

As it was, it would break her heart to let him go. Spending more time with him would only prolong the agony, make saying goodbye so much harder.

But how was she supposed to carry on with a normal life after last night? How was she supposed to…?

"So, you wanna tell us about the hickey on your neck?" Charlie teased.

Blushing, Brooke folded her hand around her throat. She'd tried to soften the clear indication of an ardent kiss with makeup, but she'd forgotten these two never missed a thing.

"It's just a scratch," she said vaguely. "What can I do?"

"You and Gavin—come on, spill the beans." Charlie grinned. "We're leading dull, married lives in comparison to yours; we need some juicy details."

"There's nothing to tell. We're together. Now. But he's leaving for Seattle soon." Brooke shrugged. "Not sure what will happen then."

"Oh, yes, I've forgotten about that," Charlie said. "I remember now Logan talking about it. He and Gavin will be taking turns to be at the office in Seattle," she explained to Lindsay. "But there's nothing that says you can't join him there, Brooke. Schools are closing, your mother would love to have Connor here to stay, and next week, you're moving to the farm anyway. If you go with Gavin…"

"Don't be silly. We've barely been together a week. This is all very new, and there is no guarantee it would last. Anyway, I have so much to do before Connor and I can move in next week. And once I'm here on the ranch, there would only be about two weeks left in which I have to finish at least another three paintings. So, there is no way I can go away now."

"You paint anywhere, don't you?" Charlie asked. "Logan has a huge apartment, as you know. There are more than enough rooms to choose from to use as a temporary studio. And then you're right there in Seattle when your exhibition opens. Why don't you…?"

"Not this time," she cut Charlie off. "I'll work faster here, even with the move. Anyway, I've already made arrangements to stay at an Airbnb closer to the gallery, for the exhibition, months ago; it's just easier for me."

The salad was done, and picking up the bowl, she motioned to the back porch. "I'll take this out."

The silence behind her followed her all the way to the table. She should never have agreed to this silly idea of a fake relationship.

They'd just finished dinner when Logan slapped Gavin on the shoulder. "So, have you decided when you'll be leaving for Seattle?"

Everybody else stopped talking and looked at Gavin and Brooke. Brooke was sitting next to Gavin but when all eyes moved in their direction, she pulled her hand out of his, stood up, and began picking up empty plates.

Gavin cleared his throat. "Actually, I've been thinking I may leave earlier than I'd originally planned. Maybe even before next weekend. I'll check flights with Anna on

Monday."

Because he was so close to Brooke, he heard her soft gasp. Without looking at him, she grabbed some plates and started walking toward the kitchen. Well, hell. He'd mentioned he might be leaving earlier. He'd thought she'd be happy about it.

Logan frowned. "Your meetings are only scheduled from the week after next—you do realize that?"

Gavin shrugged. "I know, but I thought it would give me time to see more of the city, get a feel of the office. I've never been to Seattle and I'd like to explore the city for a few days."

"That's not a bad idea," Logan said. He looked in the direction of the kitchen. "What about Brooke? I thought you two...you know."

"She...she's packing and working for her exhibition in July. At this point, I think she'd prefer not to have me under her feet, as well. So, tell me about Anna? From what I've picked up here and there from emails and phone calls, I believe she's quite a character."

Logan grinned. "I can try, but trust me, nothing I say will be able to prepare you for Anna." He launched into a description of his PA.

Gavin looked toward the kitchen door, where Brooke had disappeared minutes before. It just made sense to leave sooner than he'd planned. There was no way he could stay away from her when he lived only a few blocks away, and she'd made it clear she wasn't interested in prolonging whatever was going on between them.

Besides, it was temporary, until he left for Seattle. That she didn't want him around shouldn't have been surprising. The lines had been very clear right from the start. He couldn't change the rules now, halfway through, because he couldn't get enough of the beautiful widow.

Gavin turned his car into the street where she lived.

Brooke focused on her breathing. In and out. In and out. Connor had pleaded to stay on the ranch with her mother until the move next week, and she didn't have the heart to tell him no. Besides, she desperately needed alone-time to figure out how she was going to say goodbye to Gavin, soon, without falling to pieces.

He was leaving earlier than planned, something he'd mentioned in passing, but she hadn't thought was serious. It was obvious he'd decided if he couldn't stay for the sex, he wasn't staying.

She was not going to cry; he didn't have to know how much last night had meant to her, and he definitely should never find out she'd lost her heart to him.

The moment the engine came to a halt, she opened her door and sprinted for the front door.

"Brooke!" Gavin called out behind her, but she ignored him.

Frantically, she searched for the keys to the front door in her bag, but she couldn't find them. Behind her, Gavin's footsteps came closer.

"Let me try," he said.

"I can get my own damn keys," she grumbled.

"Of course you can. You don't need me; you've made that abundantly clear. I'll stay out of your way until I leave. Once I'm gone, you can tell everyone we're not together anymore."

"See if you can find the damn key." Upset and angry, she shoved the bag into his hands and crossed her arms. He found it immediately and unlocked the door.

Quickly, she stepped inside and held out her hand. "Thank you. The key?"

"It's best that I leave earlier."

"So you say."

"I'm...it's just..." He rubbed his face. "Babe, I'm no good to you..."

"Don't you dare say that! I don't understand how you can believe someone who has lied to you and cheated on you, but you can't see how much you mean to your sisters and…and to everyone else."

"Everyone else?"

"You keep using someone else's words to explain why you want to leave. It doesn't work, okay? Just…go."

Her eyes were bright. Tears? It couldn't be, could it? Taken aback, he stared at her. Why was she crying? He never could stand tears, something his two sisters used to their advantage time and time again while they were growing up.

"Goodbye, Gavin. I'll …" One tear spilled onto her cheek, but she wiped it away quickly. "I'll…"

And then he noticed it—the slight tremor of her lower lip. She quickly bit down on it, but he'd seen it. With a groan, he stepped inside her house, kicked the door shut behind them, and pulled her closer. "Babe…" was all he managed before his mouth found hers.

The moments his lips captured hers, the chaos inside of him subsided. This was where he wanted to be. Here. With her. And yes, he couldn't make any promises to her—he wasn't any knight in shining armor—but damn it, right now, he needed her to rescue him.

Her arms snaked around his neck, and she clung to him. Without taking his mouth from hers, he picked her up and staggered up the stairs to her room. Besides the burning desire to become a part of her as soon as possible, there was another feeling he couldn't quite define, egging him on.

In her room, he let her slide down onto the floor, his hand finding its way to a silky leg underneath the short skirt of her dress.

CHAPTER 11

The constant buzzing sound from his phone finally roused Gavin from a deep sleep. Brooke was sprawled over him, her hair covering his body. Still groggy, he picked up his phone. "What the hell?" There were three missed calls from Charlie and four from Lindsay.

Brooke stirred and opened her eyes. "What time is it?"

"Nearly ten."

She sat up quickly, combing her hair from her face. "Ten? But it can't be!"

Grinning, he leaned forward and planted a kiss on her lips. "We haven't slept much over the last two nights. Let me call one of my sisters and find out what's the crisis. Can't be Lindsay's baby—it's way too early—so it's probably another dinner they're planning."

Brooke slid off the bed. "I'll make coffee."

With his gaze following Brooke as she slipped into shorts and a top before she left the room, he dialed Charlie's number.

"Gavin, thank goodness you've finally answered!" Charlie called out. "You best get yourself over to your house; the neighbors have called several times."

"Why? Anything wrong?"

"Sarah arrived on your doorstep early this morning."
Sarah? Who was Sarah?

"Sarah, as in your last girlfriend Sarah?" Charlie said.

"Oh, that Sarah. What is she doing here?"

"Looking for you. Apparently."

"How…?" Swearing, he grabbed his jeans. Now was not the time to ask too many questions. "I'm on my way."

When he looked up, Brooke was standing in the doorway.

Pulling on his jeans, he glanced around, looking for his shirt. "You heard that?"

"That Sarah is here? I did—sorry, I didn't mean to eavesdrop. I came to get my phone; I want to check up on Connor. Well, there you have it, then—she obviously wants you back, so she's decided you're not that bad at relationships after all." She turned around and disappeared.

Dumbfounded, Gavin stared after her. Damn it to hell, what was she talking about? "Brooke!" He finally found his shirt, and pulling it over his head, he searched for his shoes.

He'd wanted to talk to Brooke that morning so they could figure out a way to stay together longer than they'd originally planned. There was nothing that said they couldn't continue their relationship even when he left for Seattle.

But now Sarah was here, and he'd have to deal with her first, find out what she wanted. And make sure she knew he wasn't interested in getting back with her ever again.

The shoes were under the bed. Cussing a blue streak, he put them on before he raced downstairs. "Brooke!" She wasn't in the kitchen or living room.

Taking the stairs two at a time, he charged back upstairs again. "Brooke!" He kept calling her name while he checked every room, but she was nowhere to be found.

His phone rang. Charlie again. He ignored it.

Damn it to hell. "Brooke—where the hell are you? We have to talk!"

Nobody answered.

Downstairs, he looked around again, but he couldn't feel her presence anywhere. Where had she disappeared to? He slipped out front and made sure the door was locked. As he rushed to his car, he took out his phone. Maybe he could send Brooke a message, tell her— Dammit, no. Messages tended to get misinterpreted, sometimes. Once he'd spoken to Sarah, he'd come back and explain everything to Brooke.

Brooke waited until she heard the sound of Gavin's SUV driving away before she went back inside the house. She'd been hiding in the garden. Sarah was here, and that could only mean one thing: she wanted him back.

Since last night, she'd tried to prepare herself to say goodbye to Gavin sometime in the coming week, when he'd leave for Seattle. Her poor heart had been valiantly trying to come to grips with the idea he was going to be away for about a month, and by the time he'd be back, everyone would've heard they weren't together anymore.

That had been bad enough. Last night's lovemaking had only intensified her feelings for Gavin. Their bodies fitted together so perfectly; they were so in sync with one another, they'd moved together like a choreographed dance.

How was she supposed to carry on with her life without him?

Sarah was here. The same Sarah who had cheated on him, who had made him feel he was not relationship material. And Gavin couldn't leave fast enough to get to her. He would probably forgive her, and she'd be the one going with him to Seattle.

Brooke swallowed the huge lump in her throat. Dammit, loving Gavin had turned her into a blubbering idiot. She was a strong, independent woman. She shouldn't simply fall apart. This thing between her and Gavin had been supposed to be temporary. Apparently, she was the one who'd forgotten all about that.

Her phone rang. Her mother. She really was the last person Brooke wanted to talk to right now, but she had to make sure Connor was okay. While she locked the kitchen door behind her, she answered the call.

"Mom?"

"Brooke, sweetie, I've heard. I'm coming to fetch you…"

"No, please don't. Thank you for caring, but I'll be okay. I'm going to switch off my phone and lock myself in. I'm going to paint for the next few days. Will Connor be okay?"

"When he's not following Logan around, he's with Blake—don't worry about him. And fortunately, my daughter-in-law and her sister are very good cooks. He's in heaven."

"Don't worry about me, Mom…"

"Of course, I worry about you. You shouldn't read too much into Sarah's visit. He hasn't invited her, and remember, the two of you are together."

The tears came out of nowhere. Furiously, she blinked them away. Her mother must never know how much she was hurting right now.

"We've…we've decided to go our separate ways, Mom. It's over. Even before Sarah's arrival. We've tried, but…well, we've tried. I'll be fine—please don't worry about me. I'll be painting until the move on Friday."

Her mother was quiet for a few moments. "I'm so sorry to hear that. Are you sure? The two of you seemed to be so in tune with one another. He can't keep his hands off of you, sweetheart—"

"I'm sure," she quickly interrupted her mother. The last thing she wanted was to be reminded of Gavin holding her hand, touching her. She swallowed down the lump in her throat. "Besides, now Sarah is here. I have to get started; I have so much to do. Give Connor a kiss from me?"

"Of course. Do you need help packing up the last of your things? I could come and help anytime."

"I will let you know. But right now, I have to finish a painting first. I'll be okay. Please don't worry about me. Goodbye, Mom."

"What can I do? You're hurting. I have to do something!"

"I've been through worse, Mom, I'm okay."

"Please remember to eat and sleep!"

"This from the woman who never sleeps or eats while she's painting?" Brooke teased.

"I don't need that much sleep nowadays. But you're still so young and beautiful. I—"

"I'll be fine, Mom. I'll let you know when I'm done."

Brooke ended the call and switched off her phone. One foot in front of the other—that was how she'd survived Adam's death. That was how she'd survive this.

But Gavin wasn't dead. Yes, but he'd left her. Literally left her for another woman.

The tears started at the same moment a huge hole opened up inside her. Taking the steps to the top floor two at a time, she didn't wipe the tears away; she let them fall.

Use the pain. Work through the pain. Paint the pain. This would be her mantra until she was finished.

By the time she had a fresh canvas on the easel and had the oils she wanted to use out, pain had penetrated every cell of her body and her face was wet with tears.

With her gaze flickering between the white canvas and the glass palette in her hand, she mixed oils. Sniffling, she wiped her face. A painting was taking shape in her mind, in her heart, in her soul. All she had to do was get it on the canvas.

Reaching out with her hand, she picked up the palette knife. She'd also use a brush for the more delicate strokes later, but first, some sharp lines. The knife slid over the canvas, leaving dark grey strokes. Frowning, she added another stroke. Grey. She seldom used greys. It was for pain, for heartache, but she'd also experienced so much pleasure over the course of the last two nights.

Pleasure. She had to get that right, as well. The next swipe of her knife left a bright, red stroke. Red. Love. Bleeding. Why was she hurting so much? Could it be she actually bled? In a trance, she looked down at herself. No, she was fine. The pain was just so unbearable.

Her hand moved swiftly, securely over the canvas. She stopped thinking and let her feelings bleed through her hand and palette knife onto the canvas until she wasn't sure where her pain ended and the painting began.

Gavin hammered on her front door. "Brooke!"

He'd been calling her and sending messages ever since Sarah had left, but all he'd been able to reach was her voicemail. She was working and had probably switched off her phone, but surely she had to hear the knocking on her door? Why wouldn't she open her door?

Stepping down from the porch, he looked up toward the second floor. The windows of the room she used as a studio were open, so she should be here. What the hell?

"Brooke!" This time he yelled. Why didn't she answer?

With his eyes on the window, he called her again on her phone. Still just a voice message. Damn it to hell. Dread was building up inside of him. Why wouldn't she talk to him?

"Brooke!" He sprinted up the steps and knocked on the door with his fist again. And waited. Nothing.

Maybe she wasn't here. Maybe she was on the ranch. He was dialing Eleanor's number as he raced back to his SUV.

"Gavin?" Different to other times, her voice was cool. Very cool.

He started his car. "Eleanor, thank goodness! Is Brooke on the ranch?"

"No."

"So where is she?"

"Not your business any longer, I believe."

Stunned, he lifted his foot from the clutch. "What do you mean?"

"That you and Brooke are not together anymore. I assume because Sarah came back. I now understand why you're leaving earlier for Seattle. Goodbye, Gavin, I don't really want to talk to you right now. You've broken my daughter's heart."

Before he could answer her, she'd disconnected the line.

What the hell? Frantically, he searched for Charlie's number and called her.

"Apparently, I've given you more credit than you deserve." Charlie didn't even greet him; her voice was ice cold.

"What the hell is going on? You're the one who called me to tell me Sarah was at my house. I can't get hold of Brooke. Do you know where she is?"

"You left Brooke this morning to rush over to Sarah, and you're wondering why you can't get hold of her? What was she supposed to think?"

"I didn't rush over to Sarah, damn it! I went over to my house to tell Sarah I was with someone else and to make sure she understands there could never be anything between us again. If I 'rushed,' it was only so that I could get back to Brooke as soon as possible. But now she's not picking up her phone."

"You also announced to everyone around the table yesterday you're thinking of leaving for Seattle earlier than planned. I saw Brooke's face afterward."

Frustrated, he rubbed his face. "It's...complicated."

"No, it isn't. Do you want to be with Brooke or not? If you can't figure it out, leave her alone. She deserves someone who loves her without any reservations. So what happened to Sarah?"

"She's left. I'm not in love with her. I never was, I've

111

realized."

"But you let the way she treated you influence your decision to never marry."

"It's not just Sarah's words that led to that decision. I wasn't there for you and Lindsay after Mom and Dad passed away."

"That isn't true, and if you're honest with yourself, you'll realize it. You did your best to make a home for us; you cooked for us over weekends, remember? And you were the one who was at my side every day I was in hospital—"

"But I missed what was going on with Lindsay! I'm her big brother. I should've known something was wrong. Even when the bastard showed up in Alisson, I wasn't here to protect her. I'm nobody's hero, Charlie. I'll be useless in a marriage."

"This is not the 1950s, my dear brother. We women are quite capable of looking after ourselves. And once you've managed to get yourself out of the pity trip you're on, you'll realize you were close by with every crisis Linds and I have ever been through. When Lindsay received the first email from Mark Taylor, you were the first person we phoned. And you immediately made plans to fly across an ocean to be here for her. What's more, you've also looked out for us when you were worried about Logan's and Blake's intentions. And in case you missed it, Brooke doesn't need a hero. She's lost a husband, picked up her life, and is making a huge success of it. What she needs is someone who loves her. But if you're still looking for excuses not to be with her, you're obviously not in love with her. When are you leaving for Seattle?"

Defeated, Gavin leaned back in the car seat. "I don't know. If Brooke doesn't want to talk to me, I may as well leave. I'll let you know when I do. It's Connor's birthday on Saturday, but I can't stay around if Brooke doesn't want to see me. Tell Connor…tell him I'm sorry I can't make it. Will you please ask Logan if he'll do the barbeque? I've promised but…"

"Will do. Love you, bro."

Long after Charlie had ended the call, he sat in the SUV, staring at Brooke's front door. She'd told everyone they weren't together anymore. The message couldn't be clearer: she didn't want to see him again.

After a while, he started his car again and drove back home, the hole inside of him larger than ever. He'd known from the start this wasn't real, that it would end. He shouldn't feel so despondent, so lost, but the idea of his life without Brooke in it had zero appeal.

CHAPTER 12

Brooke woke up with a start and lifted her head. She'd fallen asleep on her arms. Which day was it? Where was she? She'd had such a vivid dream about Gavin, she could swear he'd be right there with her. But he wasn't. He'd never be with her again.

Staring at the last painting she'd finished, still on the easel, she reached out to switch on her phone. Her mom. Connor. She'd sent texts each night for Connor, but she hadn't wanted to speak to anyone. Fortunately, her mother understood.

As she punched in her password, she heard her mom calling from downstairs.

"Brooke, sweetheart, you said you'd be all right, but it's Friday already. I'm so worried about you!" Moments later, her mom appeared in the doorway, out of breath. "Brooke!" she cried out and opened her arms. "Look at you. You haven't slept or eaten since Sunday, have you?"

Dazed, Brooke stared at her mother. Slowly, she shook her head. "I'm not sure."

Her mother hugged her tightly. "My darling girl. Look at you. You're also in desperate need of a shower and clean clothes, I think. The moving van is on its way. Logan and

Blake are coming over to help. Connor is with Charlie and Lindsay and…"

Her eyes fell on the painting still on the easel, and she inhaled sharply. "Brooke, this is…" For long minutes, she stared at it before she hurried over to the other three paintings propped up against the wall.

For the first time since she'd woken up, Brooke noticed the other paintings. She'd done them. Every stroke seemed familiar, her signature, Brooke Davidson—she'd always painted under her maiden name—was in the corner of each painting, but for the life of her, she couldn't remember actually painting them. They were like nothing she'd done before.

"Beautiful," her mother was muttering. "Just beautiful." Her eyes were filled with tears when she looked back at Brooke. "You're in love with Gavin, aren't you?"

Brooke nodded, staring at the hazy, entwined figures that had flowed out of her over the last few days. She was empty and way too tired for any filters. "I am, Mom."

"And he…?"

"Left to be with Sarah."

"Have you spoken to him?"

"No. There isn't anything left to say."

"He's—"

"Mom, I don't want to talk about Gavin, please? Not now, not before the exhibition. I have to move; I have another few paintings to finish. But I…can't talk about it now, okay?"

"But, sweetheart, please, listen—"

"Not right now, I can't bear it." Brooke got up slowly. She felt a hundred years old. She motioned to the paintings. "I'm going to take a shower. Don't let anyone touch these, please? I'll arrange to have them shipped to the gallery in Seattle. The new owners of the house won't be moving in for another week, and it's best if these stay right here until they can be sent off." She handed her phone to her mom. "Will you do me a favor, though?

116

Please delete Gavin's messages from my phone?"

Her mother took her phone before she turned back to stare at the paintings. Brooke walked out. Pieces of her heart were left behind her in that room, on those canvases. Exactly how she was supposed to continue with her heart in fragments, she had no idea.

The bed in her room was still unmade. She and Gavin had made love right here mere days before. Quickly, she shut down the memories and stripped the bed. She'd wash the sheets once she'd moved into their new home.

She vaguely remembered hearing Gavin's voice, remembered him hammering against the front door. But there was no way she could face him at that point and not blurt out how much she loved him.

Time was a wonderful healer of wounds, she'd discovered. It wouldn't be easy and it wouldn't be soon, but at some point, she was going to put last week out of her mind. The whole fake relationship had lasted about a week; she'd get over him in time.

She would miss his cooking. And his smile. Oh, and those hands...

Focusing on her breathing, she quickly undressed and stepped into the shower. Minutes later, the first tears mingled with the water before a sob escaped from deep within her.

Gavin smiled and shook hands with everyone at the office in Seattle and tried to sound like the competent new partner who knew what he was doing, but by Friday he was exhausted. It was a huge effort to look happy and excited. His heart wasn't in it. He couldn't stop thinking about Brooke, and even though he knew she probably wouldn't answer any of his many messages, he kept checking his phone. He'd sent another one earlier in the day.

Maybe he should've waited for her to calm down so

that he could talk to her and explain about Sarah before he'd left for Seattle, but it wasn't as if he hadn't tried, damn it.

He was staring out over the city from the big windows of the huge office he'd been given. This was much more than he could ever dream about. His new brother-in-law had been very generous, but Logan had also made it clear what he was expecting Gavin to do and it wasn't staring out of the window thinking about Brooke.

Logan had been curt to the point of being rude over the phone when Gavin had phoned to tell him he was leaving for Seattle on Tuesday. Logan hadn't mentioned Brooke's name, but they were both very much aware of what was not being said.

And Logan's last words, "Maybe you should stay for two months before you come back," were still ringing in his ears.

Damn it to hell—he hadn't been looking for this. He'd wanted to get his and Brooke's families off their backs when he'd proposed the fake relationship. That was all.

Turning back to his desk, he pressed his lips together. Winning over clients and making sure the business was running smoothly, he could do. Relationships, not so much. He'd leave that to his two brothers-in-law; they seemed to know what women wanted.

Minutes later, there was a knock on his door, and Anna opened the door. "Safe to come in?"

He frowned. "Of course."

Arms crossed, she studied him openly for a few minutes. He stopped short of squirming on his seat.

"Anything I can help you with?" he finally asked.

"No, just checking to make sure."

"Of what?" he grumbled.

"That you don't have horns. The interns are whispering about a new devil in the office."

Bemused, he stared at the older woman. "New devil?"

"Yes, apparently someone new in the office is going

around scaring the poor interns."

"Me, scaring interns? Where did you hear that?" But even before he'd finished the question, he remembered. Yesterday, he'd found some giggling interns at the copier, and he'd probably been shorter than he'd needed to be. But this was a workplace, damn it, not a gossip corner.

Irritated and slightly uncomfortable, he rubbed his neck. "They should stay out of the kitchen if they don't like the heat."

Still with her arms crossed, she nodded. "Ah, now I get it. You've got a woman on your mind; I should've known. You look exactly like Logan did before he realized he'd fallen in love with your sister. The question is, what are you going to do about it? If I were you, I'd start with an apology to the interns. If I'd known you better, I would have had some suggestions about the woman, but let me just say if you're this miserable without her, do something about it. At this point, you're no fun to work with."

He was on his feet, ready to tell her what she could do with her suggestions, but with a lift of her chin, she walked out.

Well, hell. He was fun. What was she talking about? Okay, maybe he'd been a tad irritable. Maybe more than a tad. Deflated, he sat down again, thinking about his behavior over the past few days. He'd been miserable and everyone probably knew it by now.

Damn it, there wasn't time for thinking about feelings and missing Brooke. He had to show his new brother-in-law he was up to sharing the responsibilities of the job. Yes, he had been thinking about Brooke, but it was only because of the way things had ended between them. He hadn't scolded the interns because of that. He'd politely asked them to stop giggling, and get on with their work.

With a sigh, he got up. Anna was right, though, he owed the interns an apology, damn it. He'd been much harsher than the situation had warranted.

It wasn't as if he was miserable without Brooke. It was

just…nothing. Absolutely nothing. They'd had a few days—she was lovely—it was logical that he'd think about her, miss her.

It didn't mean anything, though. Grinding his teeth, he went in search of the two interns. The damn hole inside of him had nothing to do with Brooke. Maybe if he kept repeating this to himself, he might actually believe it at some point.

His phoned pinged twice. Both his sisters had texted him. And their news stopped him, momentarily, in his tracks.

Brooke had misplaced her phone during her move.

Well, hell.

By Sunday evening, Brooke and Connor were in their new house on the ranch. Connor had been so excited, she hadn't thought he'd ever go to sleep, and only after the sixth story had his eyes finally drooped. She was bone weary.

In the middle of the chaos, they'd also celebrated Connor's birthday the day before. Logan had stepped in and barbequed the hamburgers, but Connor had kept asking why Gavin wasn't there. Come to think of it, her son had been talking nonstop about Gavin.

Her phone had been lost somewhere in the chaos, a blessing as far as she was concerned. She didn't want to know whether her mother had deleted Gavin's messages or whether he'd tried to reach her again. It was probably in a box somewhere and she'd hopefully find it when she finally got around to unpacking everything. She'd used her mom's phone for urgent messages with the gallery, and everyone else she needed to talk to was close by. Not that she'd seen much of her family while finishing her paintings. If the phone didn't turn up, she'd get another one at some point.

Today, everyone had helped and had pitched in to get

her and Connor settled, and most of the boxes had been unpacked. Her own clothes were still in suitcases, though, and some of Connor's things were also still boxed up, but she'd spent the day unpacking her art supplies so that tomorrow morning she could start early on a final painting for the exhibition in Seattle. Middle of July had initially sounded like such a long wait, but now there was only a week left.

She had yet to recover from all the sleep she'd lost painting over the last week, and she was yearning for a few days to simply chill, but that would have to wait until after the exhibition. The finished paintings were still back in her old house. The shipping company would be picking them up the next morning.

Once the paintings were displayed in the gallery, anyone and everyone would be able to see them. She'd never felt so exposed before, so vulnerable about her work. But then, sharing her love for nature or her passion for the environment was very different from sharing the depth of her love, the strength of her desire for another human being, with the rest of the world.

The Kiss would be included in the exhibition, as well as the first painting she'd done after Gavin had left. That one, she called *The Forever-Kind*. Nobody would understand she was talking about her love for Gavin, but then nobody needed to. Those two paintings were not for sale. She couldn't bear to ever part with either one. Big chunks of her heart had been mixed in with the oil while she'd been working on them.

In the kitchen, she got out a wineglass, poured herself some wine, and wandered through the house. It wasn't big, but it was perfect for her and Connor. He was close to the rest of his adoring family, and she was still so thrilled with the studio Logan had added. It was everything she'd always wanted in a studio. The natural lighting was just right, and Logan had also installed lights for those times she wanted to work at night.

The sun had just set, and things were settling down on the ranch. She opened the door and walked out onto the back porch. It was going to take her a while to get used to the pitch dark and the silence. Not that Alisson was a noisy town, but she'd always been aware of the heartbeat of the town, even in the middle of the night.

Earlier that day, when she'd gone back to her old house to pick up the last boxes and made sure the last paintings were shipped off, she'd spent a few minutes saying goodbye. When she and Adam had bought it years ago, as newlyweds, they'd been blissfully unaware of what life had in store for them. They'd had a good life, and a part of her would probably always miss him.

It was also in the same house she'd discovered it was possible to fall in love again, only this time, she'd fallen way harder than she'd thought was possible, and she loved so much more intensely, it frightened her.

She'd loved her husband and it had taken her a while to learn to live with the heartache of losing him, but losing Gavin… It was as if a big hand tightened around her heart, making it difficult to breathe.

But she'd never really "had" him: she shouldn't be experiencing this sense of utter loss.

Over the past few days, while moving to the ranch, Charlie, Lindsay, and her mother had taken turns trying to drop Gavin's name in conversations, but she'd walked away every time.

She didn't want to talk about Gavin or hear how much he and Sarah were enjoying Seattle. She didn't want to know how happy he was, how much he loved the woman who'd come back into his life.

"There you are." Her mother's voice brought her out of her reverie. She, Charlie and Lindsay were approaching from the side of the house.

"We've knocked, but when you didn't answer, we thought we'd find you here," Charlie said.

"We're ambushing you," Lindsay added. "Come on, I

also want a glass of wine." Taking Brooke by the arm, she marched her into the house, her mother and Charlie right behind them. "Have you listened to any of Gavin's messages, or is your phone still missing?"

"It's probably still somewhere in a box. I don't want to talk about Gavin."

But this time, her mother was not going to be ignored. "You keep shutting us down when we try to talk to you about him. There are things you don't know, things that would change your mind about him if you did. Please, just listen to us."

"Gavin is with Sarah now. I've put it behind me and I really don't want to talk about it."

Her mother pulled Brooke close and hugged her. "My dear girl, we've been trying to talk to you for days, but you keep walking away. Gavin has left for Seattle, yes, but he's on his own. I'm not sure where Sarah is, but she's not with him. He came back to you, but you wouldn't answer any of his messages or open your door for him."

Brooke froze. Her brain was struggling to make sense of her mother's words. Gavin was alone in Seattle. *Alone.* He wasn't with Sarah.

After long minutes, during which she tried to connect all the dots, she pulled herself out of her mother's embrace. There wasn't anything to connect.

"Well, the bottom line is, he's left. He obviously doesn't feel the same way I do. Besides, he has been very clear, right from the start, that he wasn't in the market for anything permanent. Anyway, he's in Seattle now and I have an exhibition to focus on. Could we please talk about something else?"

"But…" Lindsay and Charlie began simultaneously.

Shaking her head, Brooke lifted her hand. "I can't do this now, please?" she said, swallowing back the tears.

"Okay, sweetie." Her mom nodded. "But please think about what we've said?"

By the time the three women left, Brooke was

exhausted. Halfway to her room, she stopped to peek inside Connor's room. He was sleeping the sleep of the innocent. She pulled up his blankets and kissed his forehead before she went to her own room.

The room was bigger than the one she'd had in the previous house, and her mom and Charlie had placed two chairs and a coffee table in the one corner. It was a lovely home—her room was warm and cozy—but she couldn't shake the feeling something was missing.

With a sigh, she sat down on one of the chairs and closed her eyes.

Gavin wasn't with Sarah. He'd apparently sent her messages, but her phone was missing. And maybe it was all for the best. He wasn't interested in anything more permanent: he'd been very clear about that. Jumping up, she headed for the bathroom.

She still had paintings to finish, a little boy who needed her, she wasn't going to sit there and pine after a man. At some point, this heartache would have to easier to live with, surely?

CHAPTER 13

The first week on the ranch flew by way too fast. By the Monday of the second week, Brooke had finished another two paintings. She'd hardly slept or eaten, but the chaos inside her had finally settled down to a dull ache.

There was nothing inside her left to give, nothing more she could put on a canvas. She'd bled out her love for Gavin, her heartache over losing him, and had turned white surfaces into reflections of her soul. She was empty.

Waving to the van that had picked up the last two paintings, she walked out onto the front porch of her new house. She had no idea what the reaction to her new works would be, but she felt good about what she'd accomplished.

Everyone on the ranch had popped in at various times over the week to watch her progress, but only her mother had been there the night before to see the end result before the paintings had been wrapped for shipping. Her mom's eyes had been bright with tears. As an artist herself, she perfectly understood the emotion, the drive behind Brooke's paintings.

Brooke stretched her arms. She'd finally heard from Lynda Gover, the owner of the gallery in Missoula. Lynda had been so upset about Bill's behavior, she'd fired him immediately, she told Brooke. And as Brooke had suspected, she hadn't been the only artist who had problems with him.

At least Bill Norton was one less problem she had to worry about, thank goodness.

She walked down the steps and followed the footpath that led to Charlie's house. Chances were, her mom and Lindsay would also be there, and one of them would know where Connor was.

It was time to have an actual conversation with her family, for a change. Her show opened on Friday, and she was leaving for Seattle on Wednesday. It would give her time to get settled in, make up for all the sleep she'd missed, and she would have the opportunity to make sure she was happy with the exhibition.

As usual, all her family members had received an invitation to the opening night, but up to now, they'd been strangely reluctant to give her an answer whether or not they might be attending. Her mother hadn't blinked when she'd asked if Connor could stay with her. Everyone was so busy, though, and Lindsay's baby was due in two months; it was quite understandable that they didn't have the time. Strange, but understandable.

Brooke pressed her hand to her tummy. For the past few days, she'd been feeling icky, like a cold was coming on. Probably due to the fact she hadn't really had a full night's sleep since...well, since Gavin had left her. Oh, drat the man! He kept popping into her thoughts at the most inopportune moments.

As she neared the main homestead, Charlie came out on to the porch with Ellie on her arm. The little girl laughed and stretched out her arms when she saw Brooke.

"Hi, stranger." Charlie smiled as she waited for Brooke. "It's so nice to see you again. I hope we can have an actual conversation now. I noticed the truck that just left—the last of your paintings?"

"Yes, thank goodness. Now it's out of my hands."

"Well, from what I've seen, people are going to love them. They're so different to any of your previous work. Everything you've done is, of course, stunning, but what you did this time round, it's just *wow*. Your paintings are so honest and raw and powerful. I don't think anyone can look at them and not be moved."

Brooke held out her hands, and with a laugh, Ellie willingly let Brooke take her from her mother. "Oh, look at you, all smiles and big eyes," Brooke crooned. She hugged the small body and inhaled the little-girl scent. "I love babies." Smiling, she kissed Ellie on her cheek.

"So how about it?" Charlie grinned. "You're not too old for another one of your own, you know?"

Startled, Brooke handed the baby back to her mother. "Of course, I am. Anyway, no husband, no baby. I'm not brave enough to try and raise one on my own. Connor was three when Adam passed and that was hard enough. If it hadn't been for my mom, I don't know how I would've coped."

Charlie's smile slipped. "Well, if you're looking for a father for your future babies, you should really talk to Gavin…"

Brooke was ready to change the topic when someone spoke from behind her.

"Please tell me you've found your phone?"

Brooke turned around quickly. Lindsay and her mom were behind her.

"It'll be somewhere. I finally have time to unpack now."

"Why don't you just phone Gavin and talk to him?" Charlie asked.

Combing her hair back, Brooke groaned out loud. "Seriously, you guys are relentless. Okay, let me tell you what really happened between Gavin and me. We've never really dated. We decided on a fake relationship to get you to back off. You were driving both of us crazy."

A shocked silence met her words. Brooke froze. She hadn't really said that out loud, had she? But the expression on the three women's faces confirmed her fears. In her frustration, she'd spilled the beans. But maybe it was for the best.

She threw up her hands. "You were pestering us on and off since Lindsay and Blake got married. We were both so tired so of trying to explain that we were just friends, to no avail. So, we came up with the idea of a fake relationship until Gavin left for Seattle."

"And the two nights he stayed with you—was that part of the fake plan?" Charlie's smile was gone, her voice frosty.

Brooke shook her head. "No...that...that was a mistake and should never have happened. He's moved on and I've put the whole thing behind me."

"Really? Is that what your new paintings are about?" Lindsay asked. "Putting a fake relationship behind you?" She didn't even try to hide her sarcasm.

"I..." But a huge lump had formed in Brooke's throat, making it impossible to talk. She couldn't cry in front of her mother, her friends; they would know immediately...

Her mother nodded. "You love him, don't you? That's what your new paintings are about. The colors, the harsh strokes, the emotion—you're hurting because you love him, and you're under the impression you've lost him."

Both Charlie and Lindsay stared at her mother before their gazes swiveled toward Brooke.

"You love him?" Charlie asked.

"I knew it!" Lindsay declared smugly. "It was so obvious to me."

Brooke swallowed a few times before she was able to talk. "It doesn't matter what I feel. For him it was only a temporary thing. He's left."

Charlie frowned. "He had a commitment in Seattle, as you very well know. And remember, you've lost your phone and haven't even tried to contact him. You don't know what he wants to say to you. Just talk to him?"

Brooke shrugged. "There isn't anything left to say. The whole thing was built on a ridiculous notion. A fake relationship. I'm the one who forgot about the 'fake' part."

Lindsay touched Brooke's arm. "I agree with Charlie—you two should really talk."

"And say what? I've fallen in love with him?"

"Why not?" her mother asked. "What have you got to lose?"

"My dignity, for starters."

Her mom rolled her eyes, sighing dramatically. "Dignity, my dear child, is a cold bedfellow. But it's your life, your decision. Your exhibition is in a few days. You're still leaving for Seattle day after tomorrow?"

Brooke nodded as they all moved into Charlie and Logan's house.

Charlie was walking in the direction of the kitchen. The long table was already laid. "Grab a chair. I've made a quiche. I was hoping we could all have lunch together. Linds, send Blake a message to tell him we're having lunch at our place, will you?" She put Ellie in a high chair standing next to the table.

With her hand protectively over her abdomen, Lindsay also sat down. "Oh, this is a busy, busy baby."

Staring in awe at Lindsay's protruding tummy, Brooke sat down next to her. "May I?"

Smiling, Lindsay took Brooke's hand and put it on her body. "Of course. Feel it?"

Filled with wonder, Brooke felt the slight movement below her hand. She still remembered how Connor used to kick her in her side when she had been pregnant with him. The idea of having another baby had died with Adam, but oh, how she would've loved holding another one.

Just then the back door burst open, and Connor charged inside, Logan a little bit behind him. "I'm hungry!" the little boy announced as he rushed toward Brooke.

Brooke put an arm around him and pulled him close.

He was growing up way too fast.

"Why was your hand on Lindsay's tummy, Mom?" he asked.

Lindsay laughed. "Come and feel for yourself. Baby is busy today." She took Connor's hand and put it on her belly.

Inhaling, Connor snatched back his hand before he put it back. "Is that Baby?"

"That's Baby." Lindsay smiled, rumpling his hair.

"Can...may we get a baby, Mom?"

Brooke laughed. "We actually can't, sweetheart."

Connor's shoulders slumped. "Because Dad is in heaven?"

Brooke nodded. "Yes, exactly."

Connor chewed his lip. "But what if we get another dad? Can we then get another baby?"

Fortunately, the back door opened at that precise moment. Thank goodness. She had no idea what to say to Connor. She'd never even considered that he'd be thinking about a baby brother or sister.

Blake entered. He immediately went over to his wife and crouched down next to her. "How are the two of you?" His hand covered Lindsay's lying over her tummy.

Lindsay laughed and answered him. Charlie put the food on the table while the conversation flowed around Brooke, but she wasn't really paying attention.

Was Connor thinking about someone specific when he'd asked about having another dad? Could it be he was thinking about Gavin?

Her thoughts jumped around, finally settling on the one she couldn't seem to shake off. Gavin wasn't with Sarah. Was that what he'd messaged her about? She had to find her phone.

"Brooke?" Charlie handed her a plate with a big piece of quiche on it. It looked delicious, but the moment Charlie put the plate in front of Brooke and she smelled the bacon, she felt nauseous.

While Charlie dished out the rest of the quiche and sent the salad around, Brooke tried to concentrate on her breathing. It was probably the lack of sleep finally catching up on her.

She could do this. Picking up her fork, she looked down at her plate, but the next minute, she shoved back her chair, jumped up, and dashed toward the first bathroom.

The stunned silence behind her followed her all the way down the corridor. What was wrong with her? What had they eaten yesterday? She tried to remember, but she felt so sick, she only had the energy to concentrate on getting to the bathroom.

Gavin had just opened the door to Logan's apartment on Monday evening when his phone rang. It was his sister, Charlie. Closing the door behind him, he dropped his gym bag and put his laptop on the table. He ignored the call. He didn't want to talk to Charlie. He didn't want to be reminded of the fact that she now probably saw Brooke every day.

It had been two weeks since he'd flown to Seattle. Two weeks during which he hadn't heard anything from Brooke. Not a message, not a phone call. Nothing. And he was slowly going out of his mind. Numerous times, he'd begun typing another message to send to her, but apparently her phone was still missing.

He missed her. He missed her laugh, her smile, her scent, the way her face lit up when she saw him, the shade of blue her eyes turned when they made love, the curve of her neck, the hitch in her breath when he entered her—he missed everything about her.

And he missed Connor. He'd somehow gotten used to the little guy asking questions about everything. It was surprising to experience life through a child's eyes again.

But Brooke probably had forgotten all about him by

now. That was why he'd been thinking of getting his own place here in Seattle. He'd also have to tell Logan he wouldn't be moving to the ranch after all.

There was no way he could live close to Brooke every day, see her but not be able to touch her. It would kill him knowing he could never make love to her again.

His phone rang. This time it was Lindsay. And now he was worried. Why would first Charlie and then Lindsay phone him? The baby?

Quickly, he answered. "Everything okay, Linds?"

"Yes, everything is fine. How are you?"

"I'm fine—"

"So why didn't you answer my call?" Charlie interrupted.

So, the two of them were together? That could only mean one thing—they were up to something.

"What's going on?"

"We heard something very interesting this afternoon," Charlie said.

He was tired and irritated and really didn't want to have this conversation. But he knew his sisters. They wouldn't stop until they'd said their piece. "What did you hear?"

"That you and Brooke had a fake relationship. I can't believe you didn't tell us!" Lindsay admonished.

Stunned, he held the phone from his ear for a few seconds before he could answer. "She's told you?"

"Over the past week, while she was moving into her house on the ranch, she didn't want us to mention your name. About a week ago, we managed to tell her you're not with Sarah, but she had paintings to focus on so we didn't push it. She's finished now, so we confronted her this afternoon. And your little secret slipped out."

Weary, he sighed. "Well, there you have it. And let it be a lesson: don't try and play matchmaker. If you haven't kept trying to get us to be together, we wouldn't have had to resort to extreme measures."

"You should see the paintings she's finished, though.

Powerful stuff. Rips one's heart out. Anyway, why we're actually calling, is to let you know we're all flying to Seattle on Friday morning for Brooke's exhibition, so you'll have roommates for the weekend. She doesn't know we're all coming to her big opening night, and of course, you don't have to go, but you may find her new paintings...interesting. See you Friday!"

And the line went dead.

Cussing a blue streak, Gavin threw down his phone. Damn interfering sisters. They were solely responsible for this whole mess. And of course, Brooke's mom. She had been the worst.

He went over to the big windows overlooking the city. Fake relationship. Nothing about his relationship with Brooke had been fake, something he'd realized within minutes after kissing her. What he'd felt when he'd been with her was all too real.

Damn it, how could she think he'd leave her for another woman after the night they'd spent together? They'd hardly slept; they hadn't been able to get enough of each other. How could she even consider the idea he'd go back to another woman?

Rubbing his face, he walked toward the bedroom. He hadn't bothered much with cleaning up after himself. He'd have to do something about the state of the apartment before the others arrived on Friday.

As he began picking up stuff in the room he'd been using, his thoughts were, as usual, with Brooke. The painting she'd done of two people kissing—was it included in the painting for the exhibition? At the time, she was adamant she was going to paint something else over it. And the other paintings Lindsay had talked about? More kissing?

The damn woman was miles away in another state, but she was still driving him crazy. Where the hell was her phone? If she'd read his messages, she'd have known earlier he wasn't with Sarah. But damn it, she should've known it even without reading any messages from him.

CHAPTER 14

His teeth tightly clenched together, Gavin entered the gallery behind Charlie, Logan, Blake, Lindsay, and Eleanor.

He'd been at the office that morning when the rest of family had arrived for Brooke's exhibition tonight. Over the last few days, he'd steadily become more and more ticked off with Brooke and had actually decided he wasn't going to attend her opening night.

He'd tried to explain about Sarah; Brooke was the one who hadn't read any of his messages when she still had her phone, the one who wouldn't open her door when he'd just about broken it down knocking. She also hadn't made any effort to communicate with him.

That had been the least she could do, damn it, after the night they'd spent together. But no, without giving him a chance to explain, she'd concluded he was going back to Sarah—what the hell?

Why hadn't she talked to him? Okay, maybe he should've told her before he'd left to see Sarah he had no intention of ever going back to her, but Brooke should've known. They'd just gotten out of bed, making love, for crying out loud. With a sigh, he rubbed his face. Okay, in hindsight, he could see why she'd been ticked off that he'd left. In the shock of the moment, he hadn't thought through how it would look from her perspective.

So here he was, showered and dressed for the occasion, looking forward to seeing her, touching her, kissing her. His sisters hadn't even had to try to convince him to come. Brooke had him tied up in knots, and she was blithely unaware of it.

He looked down at the boy next to him. Connor had moved closer to him when they'd entered the gallery, and he now moved closer still. Smiling down at Connor, Gavin put a protective hand on his small back. There was a big crowd; he completely understood how overwhelming it might be for someone so close to the ground. Hell, he was overwhelmed.

"Oh, my darling girl outdid herself," Eleanor was saying, her hands gripped tightly in front of her. "Look how magnificent."

For the first time, Gavin looked at the paintings. His breath hitched in his throat, and for a moment, the whole room tilted around him.

Frame after frame showcased hazy figures making love. In some paintings, it was barely possible to recognize the couple, but if you looked closely, they were there—in the swirl of the paintbrush, in the stroke of the palette knife. And they were exactly as Eleanor had described them— magnificent.

As they stepped around a pillar, he searched for Brooke, but he didn't see her anywhere, and when he turned back, his gaze fell on the two paintings behind a small podium.

Inhaling sharply, his heart just about jumped out of his chest. Every single painting was something special, but these two were glorious. The one he recognized immediately was the one he'd seen in her studio of two lovers kissing. In the other one, two lovers were sitting on a bed, facing one another just like…

It took him a few moments to process what he was

looking at: she'd painted the two of them.

He remembered that particular moment when they'd been sitting just like that on her bed. The feeling of utter contentment he'd experienced then wasn't something he'd ever forget. Being there with her, in that moment, had felt so right.

"They're beautiful, aren't they?" someone observed.

He glanced toward a woman dressed in bright red who was now standing next to him. "Breathtaking."

"Unfortunately, those two are not for sale. If you're interested in buying any of Brooke's works, rather do so sooner than later; they're selling quickly. I'm the curator, by the way."

"Hello, Michelle!" Eleanor interrupted as she approached them with outstretched arms. "I see you've met Gavin. Gavin, this is Michelle Martin, owner of the gallery and curator of Brooke's exhibition. This is Gavin Wilson. You may recognize him?"

Michelle's eyes twinkled. "I have, indeed."

Gavin frowned. "What do you mean? We haven't met before, have we?"

She motioned toward some of the paintings. "No, but I've seen you before tonight."

He turned around, his gaze gliding around the room. He hadn't noticed right away, but he and Brooke didn't feature in just the one painting, but in every single one. All the paintings were about the two of them making love.

"Do you now understand why we wanted you to be here tonight?" Eleanor grinned.

"You mean you didn't know?" Michelle asked.

Well, hell. It was one thing to know Brooke had painted them; it was something entirely different to have to talk about it to a complete stranger.

He pointed toward the two paintings behind the podium. "I want to buy those two."

"As I've said…"

"I insist. Talk to Brooke. If she won't budge, tell her

I'd like to talk to her."

Michelle smiled. "Of course, but do look around. I'll see you later."

"I'm hungry," Connor said, pulling at his hand.

Gavin grinned, feeling strangely relieved. Connor being hungry, he could do something about. There were obviously things he and Brooke should talk about, but two things were making him feeling lighter somehow: he was going to see her again soon, and she'd painted the two of them. In every single painting, they were the subjects. That was what the exhibition was about.

For the first time in two weeks, the tight band around his chest had eased a tiny bit. "So am I," he said to Connor. "Let's see what we can find to eat."

Brooke took a deep breath and closed her eyes for a moment before she walked into the gallery. She only hoped she wouldn't have to rush to the bathroom again soon. The feeling of nausea she'd been experiencing since last week just wouldn't abate. The flight to Seattle had been exhausting. Normally, she bounced back quickly after she'd lost sleep while painting, but this time the lethargic feeling lingered.

She'd bought another phone at the airport. Her old one was still missing. It wasn't in any of the boxes she'd unpacked. She'd dropped off a few boxes at her mom's— those were supposed to have been filled with stuff that Eleanor had left at Brooke's studio over the years. Probably her stupid phone had ended up in one of those.

The place was packed. Relieved, Brooke looked around the big, open room showcasing her exhibition. The gallery had recently moved. The raw space on the ground level of a well-known building had been converted into a beautiful, light-filled gallery. It was located a block away from a sculpture garden, sheltered from the busy streets. There was a main exhibition salon, an art-research library where she'd spent a lovely few hours since yesterday, and this big exhibition room.

Michelle's suggestions of where to hang which paintings were spot on. Turning three hundred sixty degrees, Brooke tried to find the two paintings she felt were her best work, which Michelle hadn't yet put up when Brooke had visited that morning.

The Kiss and *The Forever-Kind* would always be close to her heart, and she couldn't bear to part with them.

Michelle, dressed in a bright red outfit, spotted her, and with a wide smile, rushed over. "Brooke, darling, I'm so glad you've arrived." She was out of breath, and with a laugh, she shook her head. "Too much excitement for someone my age. We've already sold half of the paintings, and we haven't even started yet." She grabbed hold of Brooke's hand. "I'm going to introduce you in a minute, but I have a buyer for *The Kiss* and *The Forever-Kind*. Very persistent, I must add. He wouldn't take no for an answer."

But Brooke shook her head adamantly. "Sorry, I told you, those two are not for sale."

Taking Brooke's arm, Michelle walked her over to a small podium where a microphone had been set up. "As I've mentioned, a very persistent customer. If you still refuse to sell, he wants to talk to you afterward."

Vexed, Brooke glared in Michelle's direction, but the gallery owner was already on her way to the microphone. And for the first time, Brooke noticed where Michelle had put the two paintings. They were both behind the podium where the microphone was, hanging next to one another. Oh, look—how absolutely perfect. All her irritation with Michelle and her persistent client evaporated.

The next moment, though, the room swayed around her. Oh, dear. If she could only sit down, even for a few minutes, it would help. She really didn't feel well. Frantically, she searched around her. But of course, there wasn't a chair in sight. Everyone was standing or walking around. Concentrating hard, she tried to focus on her breathing. In and out. She could do this.

As Michelle cleared her throat to get everyone's attention, the crowd moved closer, except for a lone figure at the back, Brooke noticed.

As someone tapped on a microphone, Gavin turned toward the small podium. The woman in red was speaking. Brooke had to be here, somewhere. Scanning the room, he noticed a lone figure at the back. Everyone else was moving forward, except for this person.

The guy turned his head and, in that instant, Gavin recognized him. It was that creepy guy from the gallery in Missoula, he'd bet his life on it. What the hell was he doing here? What was his name again? Bill something.

With an eye on Bill, he turned to watch Michelle talk. And there...his heart skipped a beat before it kicked him in the ribs. There was Brooke, dressed in a floor-length, soft beige dress with a deep V-neck in front and at the back, and what looked like hundreds of tiny snowflakes sprinkled all over the dress. She was breathtakingly beautiful.

Out of the corner of his eye, he noticed Bill begin moving forward. He caught Blake's eye and quickly walked closer to the ex-FBI agent who was now married to Lindsay. Maybe he was unnecessarily worried, but he didn't trust Bill, not for a second.

When Michelle began to speak, Brooke turned to look at the flamboyant woman welcoming everyone. She'd worked with Michelle before on several occasions, and she loved her passion for her work.

"Please welcome Brooke Davidson. Feel free to ask questions!"

Loud applause followed as Brooke walked toward the

microphone. Several journalists would also be attending the opening tonight. Being the center of attention was not something she felt comfortable with; it was the part of her job she could really do without. Over the years, though, she'd come to appreciate that buyers of her work wanted to know something about the artist whose works they were acquiring.

As she took her place in front of the microphone, her gaze fell on the person she'd just seen hovering at the back. Her breath left her body in one swoosh as she recognized him. It was Bill Norton, the manager of the gallery in Missoula. A sick feeling of dread settled in her tummy. He'd been fired from his job, so what was he doing here? Probably up to no good, of that she was fairly sure.

As she opened her mouth to speak, Bill swiftly began to move forward in her direction, a nasty smile on his face.

Squaring her shoulders, Brooke began to talk. Bill Norton was not going to spoil her opening night. "A big round of applause for Michelle, please. You've outdone yourself, thank you. It's always such a pleasure to work with you."

As everyone clapped, Brooke searched the crowd for Bill again. He was still slowly moving forward, forcing his way through the crowd, inch by inch. Frantically, she looked around. Surely there had to be security guards somewhere?

Gavin had his eyes on Bill and followed him as he slowly advanced toward Brooke. Blake touched his shoulder, and Gavin looked at him. Blake motioned that he was going to go around the crowd toward the front. There hadn't been time to explain much, but Blake had caught on quickly that there was a problem and Brooke could be in danger. That had been all he'd needed to know.

Nodding, Gavin turned back and tried to find Bill. He wasn't where he'd spotted him previously. Where the hell had he gone?

Dread settling on his stomach, he frantically searched the crowd. There he was. Bill wasn't hurrying, but he was steadily moving closer and closer toward Brooke.

Brooke's hands felt clammy, her heart was racing, and for a minute, the whole room tilted precariously. Oh, my goodness, she couldn't be sick now; it would be a disaster.

With an eye on Bill and focusing on her breathing, she began to thank everyone. She had to get this over with as soon as possible. "Thank you for being here tonight, it means the world to me."

Bill had stopped moving for the moment; there was a solid line of people in front of him.

"Please have a drink and something to eat and enjoy the evening with us."

She was really not feeling well. If she didn't sit down soon, she was going to keel over.

"Ms. Davidson, a question?" someone asked. Brooke recognized him. A journalist.

Swallowing, Brooke tried what she hoped was a smile. "Of course."

"Like all your work, these are beautiful but they're so different from what you've done before. We're used to your landscape paintings, your commentary on the environment, but all of your paintings here feature the same couple over and over?" The journalist grinned. "Anything you want to share with us?"

Keeping her smile in place, she gave him a vague answer. "It's always a good idea to break the experience of observing a work of art into two different categories: formal and content. All art, whether it's visual art, music, film, literature or poetry can be appreciated in terms of its form and its content. The formal observation is about the artwork's physical features and characteristics whereas the content observations…"

Her eye caught Bill's again. He'd managed to move closer to her and was now about four rows from the front. "Anyway, we ask questions about the meaning of the work, the artist's intentions, and how the art makes us feel when we look at it."

Bill was still approaching, his gaze never leaving her.

" So there is no right or wrong way to appreciate a work of art—everyone would have a different interpretation."

"Any more questions?" She really hoped not, but the next minute, Bill's hand shot up.

"So, Brooke…" It was immediately clear he'd had too much to drink. With his gaze on her, he swayed forward until people in the second row from her stopped his progress. Irritated, he tried to move past them, but nobody paid him any heed.

Time for her to escape. "Thanks again to Michelle for making this possible. Enjoy yourselves!"

Michelle was right behind her and took Brooke's place when she stepped away. With a last glance over her shoulder in Bill's direction, Brooke hastened to the bathroom. Hopefully, she'd make it before she was sick—and before Bill could reach her.

The moment Brooke left the podium, Gavin hurried forward in her direction, but the crowd was dispersing, and everywhere he turned were people. Where the hell had she gone to now? He'd just looked away for a moment, and now he couldn't see her.

And then he saw Bill staggering in the direction of the bathrooms. He had to be going after Brooke.

Frantically, he looked around for Blake, but he couldn't see him either. Muttering an excuse, he elbowed his way through the people standing in his way, and as soon as he could, he began to jog in the direction where he'd last seen Bill.

Just as Brooke opened the restroom door, a clammy hand on her shoulder stopped her. She didn't have to turn around to know who it was. His breath gave him away. Bill freaking Norton.

Fed up with him, with feeling sick, she turned to glare at him. "What do you want, Bill?"

He got hold of her elbow, and swearing, he forcefully pulled her toward him. "You got me fired," he snarled.

His mouth was moving, but she couldn't hear what he was saying. She was going to be sick. Frantically, she tried to pull away, but Bill had a surprisingly tight grip on her arm.

"You got yourself fired, you idiot. Let me go!"

"There is no one to rescue you this time. Where's lover-boy now?" Sneering, he began pulling her toward the exit of the building.

With all her might, she stepped on his foot, and with her last bit of energy, she pushed him away from her. He stumbled, giving her the opportunity to pull her arm out of his grip.

Out of breath, she quickly turned around to flee, but she was stopped by an immovable object. Reassuring arms folded around her and pulled her close.

"I'm sorry, Brooke, I know you don't want me to take over, but that's exactly what I'm going to do right now."

Stunned and so relieved, she stared up into the last face she'd thought she would see that night—Gavin. He was here, just when she'd needed him most. Out of breath, she leaned into his embrace.

"Do we have a problem here?" someone asked behind her. Someone who sounded an awful lot like Lindsay's husband, Blake.

She turned around, just in time to see Blake, Lindsay,

144

Charlie, Logan, her mother, and Connor rushing forward.

"Mom!" Connor cried. "Surprise!"

While Brooke hugged her son, Blake got hold of Bill's arm and steered him toward the exit. Sputtering and swearing, Bill looked back at Brooke over his shoulder, but without letting go of Brooke's hand, Gavin took a step in his direction. Bill closed his mouth, his shoulders slumped.

"What on earth was that all about?" her mother asked.

"I..." Brooke began but the next minute, she sprinted for the bathroom. She was going to be sick.

ELSA WINCKLER

CHAPTER 15

Dumbfounded, Gavin stared at the door of the restroom. Eleanor, with Connor clutching her hand, Charlie, and Lindsay had run after Brooke, but he had no idea what was going on.

Logan, who had also been staring at the door, rounded on him. "What the hell happened? Who was that guy?"

Tearing his gaze away from the door, Gavin told Logan what he knew about Bill.

"What the hell? Why didn't Brooke tell me about it?"

"You know her—she insists on handling her own problems."

Clearly frustrated, Logan sighed. "Yeah, I know. After Adam's sudden passing, she struggled to get the estate settled, and since then…"

Gavin nodded. "She's told me about it."

Logan raised an eyebrow. "She has, has she? I've heard you guys only had a fake relationship. I didn't realize that means you've also shared intimate details."

"There is nothing fake about the way I feel about her."

At that moment, the door of the restroom opened again. Eleanor and Connor came out. "Logan, Gavin, could you take Connor home, please?"

"Of course, Mom." Logan took Connor's hand. His voice dropped. "Brooke?"

"She'll be okay in a minute. Probably just nerves. We'll stay until she can leave." She looked around. "Where is Blake?"

"He...uhm...escorted Bill outside," Gavin said, but he didn't elaborate in front of Connor. He crouched down so that he could look the little boy in the eye. "Are you still hungry?"

Connor nodded, his gaze shifting to the restroom door.

"So am I. What do you say we go and look for the biggest hamburger we can find?"

"What about my mom?" Connor's lip trembled.

Gavin picked up the boy. "She has to stay to talk to all these people who want to buy her paintings, but by the time we would have had our hamburgers, she'll be back."

"And Uncle Logan is going with you, sweetie," Eleanor said and kissed Connor.

Gavin had so many questions about Brooke, but he didn't want to upset Connor any further.

Logan smiled at Connor. "Come on, I've just realized I'm also starving."

Gavin handed the boy to Logan. "Just give me a minute. I'll meet you outside." There was one more thing he had to do before he could leave.

Brooke finally felt human again. She couldn't remember ever feeling so sick before. There was the time when she'd been pregnant with Connor, but that had been in the mornings only. And had she felt this bad? Didn't seem possible. And on top of feeling sick, the upsetting incident with Bill Norton had just made everything worse.

Not to mention the fact that Gavin had appeared like a knight in shining armor, just when she'd needed him most.

She touched Lindsay's hand. "Will you please thank Blake for me? I don't know what Bill thought he could accomplish here tonight, but I was very grateful for your husband's help."

Lindsay smiled. "It was all Gavin. He saw the guy, recognized him, and asked Blake to help. You don't have to worry about that creep again, Blake would've made sure of that."

The door opened, and Michelle popped in. She'd been in earlier but had left when she'd seen how sick Brooke was feeling. "How are you doing now? Up to facing your fans again?"

"Yes, thanks for the apple juice. I'm much better now, Michelle."

Her mom handed her a lipstick. "You're still very pale."

When Brooke looked in the mirror, she groaned. "Oh, my goodness, I look like a ghost. I can't remember ever feeling this sick. Must be something I've eaten."

She turned around in time to catch a look her mom shared with Charlie and Lindsay, but before she could ask what that was about, Michelle was ushering her outside.

"We have to talk about the two paintings you don't want to sell," Michelle said.

"I told you…"

Michelle chuckled. "Well, my dear, I don't know what to tell you. The client is very, very insistent. He'll probably contact you. But come on, there are journalists waiting to take pictures and talk to you."

"Just a moment," Brooke said, and looked back at her mom, Charlie, and Lindsay. "You guys are, of course, welcome to stay, but I'm really okay now. I'm so happy you're here. I won't even ask why you didn't tell me you were all coming to the opening night. Let's meet somewhere for lunch tomorrow?"

"But now that we're all here, why don't you come with us to Logan's place?" Charlie asked.

Because she wasn't ready to face Gavin yet. Brooke shook her head. "I'll probably be here until late tonight, and the Airbnb is walking distance. Lunch, tomorrow? I'll message you." And with a wave of her hand, she followed Michelle.

Connor had finally fallen asleep while Gavin read him a story. He'd kept asking about his mother, and it was only when Gavin settled next to the little boy with a storybook that Connor had closed his eyes.

As Gavin pulled the door closed behind him, he heard the women's voices. Brooke. His feet carried him all the way to the living room even before he'd realized he was moving. He couldn't wait to see her.

"...very happy with the exhibition," Eleanor was saying.

Gavin looked around. "Where's Brooke?"

The women shared a look. "Probably at the exhibition. She's staying at an Airbnb close to the gallery. She was still talking to people when we left," Eleanor said.

Gavin pointed toward Eleanor, Lindsay, and Charlie. "So what was that look?"

"What look?" Lindsay asked, winking at Charlie.

"You know what look," Gavin nearly shouted. He inhaled deeply. "What's wrong with Brooke? And where is she staying?"

Eleanor grinned. "Finally, he's asking the right questions."

Charlie stepped closer to him and hugged him. "We don't know what's wrong with Brooke. She thinks it was something she's eaten. We...have our own idea. I've texted you her address, although she may still be at the venue."

He was still staring at Charlie, trying to read between the lines, when Lindsay dangled her phone in front of him. "An Uber driver is on his way. The rest is up to you. Don't mess it up, okay?"

Just then, the front door opened and Blake stepped inside. Lindsay, hand on her tummy, got up and held out her arms. "I'm so glad you're back. Everything okay?"

Blake hastened forward and embraced his wife. "Everything is fine. I was just reminded of the whole bad experience you had with Mark Taylor."

"He's in jail, and I'm safe because I've got you," Lindsay murmured, hugging her husband.

"Thanks for your help tonight, Blake," Gavin said.

Blake kept an arm around his wife as he turned to look at Blake. "You've got good instincts. You reacted when someone else wouldn't have seen trouble was brewing. Brooke is safe tonight because of you."

"I didn't really do anything…"

Blake shook his head. "You saw the bad guy; you made the call. You did what your instincts told you to do, and because of that, we could intervene before he did something nasty."

"The Uber driver is here," Lindsay announced.

Gavin nodded. "Thanks."

Logan stepped forward. "You hurt her. You'll have to deal with me."

Gavin nodded curtly. "I'll make sure no one ever hurts her again, that I can promise you."

Eleanor chuckled. "Of course, you will, dear. She's special to you."

As Gavin left, he gnashed his teeth. What the hell was so damn funny?

Brooke stepped out of the gallery onto the pavement outside and lifted her face toward the sky. It was a clear night but because of all the city lights, she couldn't really see the stars. Pulling her shawl around her, she waited for the Uber to pick her up.

Michelle was ecstatic about the exhibition, the paintings had all been sold, and Brooke had also received several commissions. She should be dancing for joy and with her family to celebrate a successful opening night. Instead, here she was, on the verge of tears.

Irritated with herself, she wiped her eyes. She had nothing to cry about.

"Brooke. Babe."

She turned her head and blinked, but when she opened her eyes, he was still standing right in front of her. Gavin. And he'd called her babe.

"Gavin."

"I have to talk to you. Have you eaten? We can go somewhere to eat or have a drink or just coffee…"

She took his hand. "Come with me. An Uber is supposed to pick me up. Let me just cancel it."

Quickly she cancelled her ride, her fingers not quite steady. In silence, they walked the short distance to the apartment she was renting. At the door, she took the key out of her bag and handed it to him. There was no way she'd be able to unlock it.

When he'd opened the door, she stepped inside and switched on the light.

Behind her, she heard the click of the door being locked.

"Brooke…"

But she didn't want to talk tonight. Turning toward him, she slipped her hand behind her back and slid down the zipper.

His eyes never left hers, and only when the dress dropped in a pool at her feet did he step forward and pick her up. Her arms went around his head, and she buried her face in his neck. Inhaling his scent deeply into her lungs, she began to undo the buttons of his shirt.

His heart was hammering away at the same frantic speed her own was beating. She had no idea what was going to happen afterward, but right now, she was going to make love to this beautiful man one more time.

In the small bedroom, Gavin put her down slowly. A

pale pink bra with matching panties was all she was still wearing. And a soft smile. A beautiful, welcoming, soft smile.

Without taking his eyes from her, he quickly got rid of his clothes. "Twenty-four hours ago, I didn't think I'd ever be able to touch you again like this." He undid the clasp of her bra and cupped her breasts. "Have these missed me?" He chuckled.

Her breath hitched in her throat; her head fell back. "Sensitive, so sensitive," she whispered.

His lips were on her neck, frantically feeding, exploring every inch of her soft skin while his hands gently loved her gorgeous breasts.

His mouth slid down her upper body, reveling in the satiny texture of her skin until he could fold his lips around a rock-hard nipple.

"Gavin." Her cry broke on a sob. Her fingers were in his hair, urging him on.

They fell onto the bed, his mouth still feasting on her softness. His hands were free to roam over her body, finding every trigger spot he remembered.

And at long last, his fingers slipped beneath the satin of the last barrier where her heat welcomed him.

With a cry, her body tightened like a bow, and she reached the first crest. Beautiful, she was so, so beautiful.

But he wanted more, so much more. Eagerly, he nibbled, sliding over toned lines while his hands tried to get rid of the small satin triangle. But it wouldn't budge, and with a swift flick of his hand, he tore it from her body.

"You can't keep doing that!" she scolded, out of breath, and reached for him. "This is the second time."

"I'll buy you a dozen, but I'm not finished with you yet, babe." He grinned, and with his eyes on her, his mouth closed over her heat. Inhaling her essence, he made love to her with his hands, his mouth, his body.

Only when the warmth of her skin nearly burned his fingers did he lift himself above her. "Look at me." With her blue eyes dark with desire on him, he thrust forward.

When he entered her and she closed around him, the chaos of the last few weeks settled down at last. And in that instant, he knew why: he loved her. Deeply, irrevocably, passionately. Why had it taken him so long to discover something so obvious?

Like every other time he'd been with her, she quickly matched his rhythm. He was with her every step of the way until they crested together.

CHAPTER 16

Brooke slowly opened her eyes. It had to be Saturday morning already because the sun was up. She still wasn't quite awake, but a deep joy filled her to the brim. Gavin cradled her against his chest. She was happy, blissfully so, her hand contentedly spread out over a warm, sexy body.

Something moved against her leg. Smiling lazily, she looked up to him while her hand disappeared under the sheet. Her eyes widened. "Again?"

Folding his arms around her, he pulled her up so that their mouths were nearly touching. "I always want you, babe. Always." His mouth captured hers in a searing kiss.

Her heart sighed. She loved this man, there was no denying it. After long minutes, she lifted her head. "I have a confession to make."

"Yeah?" He combed back her hair, his fingers lingering against her face. "So have I."

"You wanna go first?"

"Sure. My confession is simple: I don't want a fake relationship with you."

She froze and pulled away quickly. "O-kay?"

Grinning, he lifted himself on his elbow. "I want a real relationship this time." Bending down, his lips teased hers.

"I never want to be without you again. What did you want to confess?"

But he kissed her then.

"My toes are curling," she whispered, before a strong wind picked her up and she soared again, losing all ability to speak or think.

In the end it was nearly time for dinner before they arrived at Logan's place. Charlie had left Gavin a message earlier, urging him to persuade Brooke to also move to Logan's place and to tell him she was preparing lunch.

They'd meant to be on time, but he couldn't get enough of her. It was nearly six before they'd finished packing her things. While she settled the bill, he'd called an Uber. He'd, of course, offered to pay for her stay at the Airbnb, but with one lift of her chin, he got the message— there was no way she was going to allow him to do that.

Gavin had Brooke's hand in his as they walked toward the front door of Logan's apartment. Being with Brooke made sense; nothing had ever felt so right.

As he opened the door, he remembered. "I still don't know what you wanted to confess. We've been so...busy, all day..." He couldn't stop the grin.

Smiling, she snuggled against him. "And every time I tried to talk, you kissed me!"

He bent down. "I like kissing you." As always, being this close to her, his lips wanted hers again.

The front door flew open. "They're kissing again!" Connor groaned over his shoulder to the rest of the party behind him.

Brooke laughed and crouched down in front of him. "I've missed you. Are you okay?"

Connor threw his arms around his mom's neck. "I've missed you, too. There's lots of food."

Laughing, Brooke stood up and took Connor's hand. Connor looked around to Gavin and held out his other hand.

Gavin took the small hand in his before he looked at Brooke. Her eyes were suspiciously bright. So what was a guy to do but kiss her again?

"Again?" Connor sighed as they walked into the living room where the rest of the family were waiting.

Gavin ruffled Connor's hair. "Told you: I really, really like your mom."

Connor stopped. "Mom, if Gavin likes you, can he be my new dad? And if I have a new dad, then what about a—"

Brooke quickly put a hand over Connor's mouth. The last thing she wanted Gavin to hear was her son talking about babies. "Uncle Gavin and I like each other, but that doesn't mean he's going to be your new dad, okay?"

Gavin stared down at the two people who had become such an integral part of his life over the past few weeks. A dad. He waited for the usual panicky feeling he usually experienced whenever anyone mentioned kids, but this time there wasn't any. Just a deep contentment.

Charlie, with Ellie on her arm, stepped closer and handed him the baby. "I'm so glad you're finally here. Uncle Gavin, please? Logan is helping me put dinner on the table. Of course, we've actually been ready for you guys since lunchtime."

Grinning, Gavin took the baby. "We were busy."

"I bet you were."

While Gavin greeted everyone else, he was aware of Ellie's big eyes watching him the whole time.

"Hello." He grinned down at the baby and was rewarded with a wide, toothless smile.

Eleanor moved closer and touched Ellie's cheek. "You're such a cutie pie, aren't you?" She held out her hands to take Ellie, but the little girl put her head against Gavin's chest, apparently quite content to be in his arms.

Eleanor grinned. "Mmm, you clearly have a way with the ladies. You and Brooke?" she asked in a softer voice.

He scanned the room. Brooke was talking to Lindsay, but her gaze was on him. He winked; she blushed. Grinning, he looked back at Eleanor. "We've dropped the 'fake' in our relationship."

"And?"

"And we're together now."

"And?"

While he rhythmically rubbed Ellie's small back, he frowned. "Not sure what you mean?"

Eleanor rolled her eyes. "Seriously. I can't believe you're so dim. Of course, there's an 'and.'"

"Like what?"

"I don't even know where to begin. Okay, do you love her?"

"Of course I love her."

"And you've told her?"

"Well, not in so many words, but—"

"We women need to hear the words. The exact words. Charlie, tell him."

For the first time, he noticed his sister was openly listening in on their conversation. "Tell me what?"

"You love her?" Charlie whispered.

"Yes, damn it, of course, I do."

"Took you long enough to realize it," she teased while covering Ellie's ears with her hands. "No swear words in front of the kids, Uncle Gavin." She glanced over her shoulder at Brooke. "Tell her. Use your words. Make sure she knows exactly how you feel about her."

Eleanor nodded. "See?"

"Shall we eat?" Logan interrupted, putting an arm around Charlie. "What's going on?"

"He loves your sister." Charlie grinned.

"Really?" Logan drawled, the beginning of a smile hovering around his lips. "Many things make sense now."

Gavin handed Ellie back to Charlie. "Yes, really. Let's eat." And he quickly walked over to where Brooke and Lindsay were still talking. He had to touch her; he had to make sure he wasn't dreaming any of this.

Lindsay lifted her glass filled with water. "I can't wait to toast the two of you with real champagne, but for the moment, water will have to do. To Gavin and Brooke— I'm so happy for you."

As everyone lifted their glasses, Lindsay leaned closer to Gavin. "So have you told Brooke how you feel about her yet?" she asked Gavin with a wink.

Gavin shook his head. "There hasn't exactly been time. We've just arrived…"

"I have this wonderful idea what you should do—"

Grinning, he shook his head. "I have my own plans."

Lindsay frowned. "Maybe you should tell me?"

"Relax, sis. I know Brooke. I know what to do."

Sometime during dinner, Gavin disappeared. The one minute he was by her side, and the next, he'd disappeared. Brooke looked down at the lovely food Charlie had prepared; she'd been so hungry, but oh dear, the nausea was back. What was wrong with her? Last night around the same time, she'd also felt so sick.

When they were back in Alisson, she should make an appointment to see the doctor. She hadn't been for a check-up in a while. But she'd been working hard over the past two weeks while not sleeping or eating enough. Hopefully, once things were back to normal, she'd feel her old self.

Except she didn't think she'd ever be able to feel her old self after last night and today. Something had changed deep within her, forever. She couldn't picture a future without Gavin in it. They hadn't made about any plans, but she wanted to be with him, even if he didn't want to get married.

"Brooke, sweetheart, will you come with me?"

When she looked up, Gavin was standing next to her, holding out his hand.

She put her hand in his and got up. For a moment, the room around her tilted and she grabbed hold of the chair. Oh, dear. "Sorry, I—" She bolted for the room she usually used when staying at Logan's apartment.

Behind her, she heard quick footsteps—probably her mom or Charlie or Lindsay or all three of them, but she couldn't be bothered—she needed to get to a toilet, and quickly.

She just made it to bathroom. What on earth was wrong with her? Afterward, her hands shaking, she washed her face and stared at her pale face in the mirror. She should make an appointment with the doctor, sooner rather than later.

When she finally left, the other three women were waiting for her on the bed.

"How are you feeling?" her mom asked.

She sat down on the bed before she leaned back against the pillows and closed her eyes. "I'm better, thanks. Just give me a minute. I haven't slept well over the past few weeks…"

"You think that's the only problem?" Charlie asked.

"I'll make an appointment with the doctor when we're back." She opened her eyes to catch the other three women grinning and sharing a look again. She sat up. "What's with the look? This is the second time you guys smile and look at each other. Come on, spill."

"You haven't been feeling well over the past few days, have you?" Lindsay asked.

"No, but as I've said, I've worked all hours and I haven't slept enough."

"Have you ever felt nauseous before when you've lost sleep while painting?"

Shaking her head, Brooke got up. She was feeling much better, and Gavin wanted to talk to her. "Can't say that I have. Probably something I've eaten. I have to go—

Gavin…"

Eyes twinkling, Charlie interrupted her. "Or something you've done?"

"What do you mean?"

Her mother laughed. "Brooke, sweetie, don't you think you're…I don't know, maybe pregnant?"

The word "pregnant" exploded in Brooke's brain. Staring at her mother, she tried to remember. She couldn't be, could she? They'd used protection every time, hadn't they? Oh, dear. There had been the one time when he couldn't get to the package on the bedtable quickly enough… She'd forgotten all about it, but now…

It took another few seconds for her scrambled brain to do the arithmetic and count the days. "Oh, my goodness, you're right. I could be pregnant. I'm probably pregnant. Never thought I'd utter those words again."

Charlie and Lindsay clapped their hands, and her mom's eyes were wet with tears.

But a feeling of dread settled in the pit of her stomach. Quickly, she sat down on the bed again. "What do I tell Gavin? He doesn't want to get married; he was very adamant about that."

"Only because he thinks he's not capable of looking out for his loved ones," Charlie said. "Talk to him about it."

Frowning, Brooke stared at Charlie. "He's mentioned something like that before. He told me he's hopeless at any kind of relationship, and he's not marriage material."

"Mostly because he thinks he wasn't there for me," Lindsay said. "After our parents passed away and Charlie was in hospital, he was juggling a job and looking after her. It was during that time I met Mark. He still blames himself for not seeing sooner that I was in trouble."

"Well, last night he was the hero," Brooke said.

Lindsay grinned. "Mention that when you tell him about the baby."

"I don't even know for sure whether I'm pregnant."

"We can find out easily enough," Charlie said and took out her phone. "Let me order a test for you; it'll be delivered..."

But Brooke shook her head. "No, thanks. I...I'll go and get something tomorrow morning. Right now, I'm beat and I...need time to...I need time. I can't talk to Gavin right now. Mom, will you tell Gavin and Connor...?"

Her mother got up. "Go and have a lovely bath. I'll tell Gavin you'll see him tomorrow. And I'll take care of Connor. Oh, and by the way, I've found your phone. It was in one of the boxes you dropped off at my place. It's been charged." With a big smile, she handed it over.

Brooke heard the other women leave, but her eyes were on her phone.

Quickly she scrolled to Gavin's messages. Had her mother deleted them? Her heart kicked against her ribs. No, she hadn't. Every single one he'd sent was still there.

With her phone in her hand, she lay back against the pillows and began to read his texts, one by one. She had to remember to thank her mother.

CHAPTER 17

Gavin was pacing the short corridor in front of the bedroom Brooke, her mother, and his sisters had disappeared into what felt like hours ago.

"What the hell is going on in there?" Frustrated, he stared at Blake and Logan who, by the looks of things, were on the third bottle of champagne.

"I don't know"—Logan chuckled—"but you should probably prepare yourself. It's never good when they're together like that. All sorts of things get planned."

"Like what?"

"Like weddings," Blake said with a straight face.

"Weddings?" Gavin repeated and deflated, he sat down. "I…" He patted his pocket. "I have my mother's ring. Charlie had brought it with her, but I'm not sure whether I should ask Brooke to marry me."

Logan's eyes narrowed.

"I want to," Gavin added quickly. "Believe me, there is nothing I want more than to always be with her and Connor, but I'm not good at relationships. What if I can't protect her? And what about…?" He motioned toward the little boy playing in the corner with his cars. "Am I really the best 'new dad' he could get?"

Blake shrugged. "Probably not. But if you love her, nothing else matters."

The bedroom door opened, and this time, both his sisters and Eleanor walked out.

Eleanor walked over to Gavin. "Brooke will see you tomorrow morning."

"Is she okay?"

Eleanor patted his arm. "She'll be fine. It's been a long day—give her time."

Gavin stared at the closed bedroom door. This was not how he'd wanted the day to end. Deep in thought, he walked toward the front door.

"Where are you going?" Lindsay asked.

"Out. I have my key. I'll be back later."

It was just before six the next morning when Brooke slipped out of the apartment. She was on her way to the convenience store close to the apartment building.

She'd hardly slept the night before, after reading all of Gavin's messages, even though she'd been so tired. Afterward, she'd wanted to talk to him or send him a message, but in the end, she knew she had to know for sure if she was pregnant or not before she told him how she felt about him.

He wanted to talk to her. Exactly what about, she didn't know, but he'd said he never wanted to be without her again. Whether he was talking marriage or whether he wanted them to live together wasn't clear at this point, but she had to tell him about the baby. If there was a baby.

She took the stairs. It gave her more time. Ridiculous, really. The sooner she knew whether or not she was pregnant, the better for all concerned.

A baby. She and Adam had talked about having another one, but after he'd passed, she'd put the idea out of her head. She'd had her chance at love; she had a son. *Not many people fell in love again,* she'd argued.

And then she'd met Gavin.

What he made her feel... Smiling, she skipped down the last few steps and nearly missed the last one. Out of breath, she steadied herself against the wall. Oh, my goodness, she could be carrying a new life inside her; she should be more careful.

"Babe, are you okay?" A very worried-looking Gavin had just entered the building and was rushing toward her.

"I'm fine." She smiled and walked into his arms.

He hugged her tightly against him. "I've been so worried about you. I wanted to talk to you last night, and then, when your mother said you wanted to be alone, it freaked me out. Are you really okay?"

She pulled away slightly. "I read your messages last night. Your previous messages, the ones you sent me when you left me to go to Sarah. I read those, and I listened to all the others."

"I didn't leave you to go to Sarah, I—"

She put a hand on his lips. "I know. I'm sorry I hadn't listened to them before, but I was so sure you were going back to her, and I didn't...I couldn't bear to hear that."

Gavin cupped her face. "I'll never leave you, Brooke. That was what I wanted to talk to you about last night. I—"

"Before you say another word, there is something I have to do first. Will you wait for me in my room?"

"No!" he cried out, his eyes a bit wild. "I've been walking the streets all of last night, missing you, wanting to be with you. I told you yesterday I never want to be without you again—don't send me away. Whatever you need to do, I'll do it with you."

"Why?"

"Because I love you, damn it. I've told you before, I'm nobody's hero, and I don't know—"

Joy burst open inside of her, but she cut him short. "Don't you dare say that ever again."

He frowned. "That I love you? But..."

165

"That you're nobody's hero. You're my hero. You've rescued me twice now even when I didn't want your help. And that's not all. You knew what to do when I burned my hand with the tea, you get me to places on time, you find my phone when I have no idea where it is, and you're so good with Connor—he's mad about you." She tilted her head. "You really love me?"

He kissed her. Hard, urgently. "Yes, damn it, I love you. Probably since the first moment I laid eyes on you, but definitely since the first time I kissed you."

"I'm so happy to hear that."

"What about you?"

She grinned. "What about me?"

His eyes darkened. "The words, babe. I need to hear the words."

"I love you, Gavin Wilson. I loved you since forever."

A huge grin appeared on his face and he kissed her again. "That's such a corny line."

Laughing, she took his hand in hers. "I've got lots more. Are you happy?"

"I'm very happy."

"You may not feel the same way in about fifteen minutes."

"What do you mean?"

"You'll see."

Gavin wasn't sure where Brooke was taking him, and he really didn't care. He was with her, touching her, looking at her. Just a few minutes ago, he still had no idea whether she was ill...

"You still haven't told me why you keep disappearing into bathrooms."

They entered a convenience store. "We're about to find out."

"What are you talking about?"

But she ignored him while she looked through the

display of goods. She reached out to pick up a small, rectangular box. "Here we go. This is what we need."

His eyes dropped to the lettering on the outside. In big, black, bold letters was the brand name, and just below it, in red the words: Pregnancy Test.

He lost his breath.

Brooke caught his arm. "Gavin! Breathe, babe, breathe. And please know, it's totally okay of you're not ready for this. I am, though. I've always wanted another baby, and now she or he will be yours, but of course, I'll understand if you—"

"You're carrying my baby?" he interrupted her, cupping her face.

"Well, we're about to find out."

He grabbed the box from her, and with her hand in his, marched toward the cashier. "I'm paying for this."

"Okay."

She was quiet all the way up the elevator back to the apartment. Nobody else was up yet, and he followed her to her room.

"So how does this work?" he asked as she took the box from him.

Not quite meeting his eyes, she turned away. "Give me a minute." She disappeared into the bathroom.

He waited. And waited. What felt like hours later, he knocked on the door. "Brooke?"

The door flew open. She was holding something in her hand.

"What?"

Her eyes were filled with tears, her lower lip trembling. She lifted her hand and showed him a what looked like a white stick.

"What is this?" he asked, staring at the two small windows on a small screen on the stick. On the one was a vertical line and on the other a plus sign.

He inhaled sharply. "You're pregnant? Is that what it says?"

She nodded, her eyes wet with tears. "That's what it says."

Joy exploded in his chest, and laughing, he picked her up. "You're pregnant!"

Her arms slipped around his neck. "Does that mean you're happy about it?"

"Of course, I'm happy about it—you're carrying our baby!"

"You've said you're never getting married."

"I've said a lot of stupid things. But, babe, doing life with you, making babies with you—I've never thought—"

The door burst open. "Brooke…" Charlie, Lindsay, and Eleanor rushed in.

Reluctantly, Gavin put Brooke down. This damn interfering family was everywhere.

Eleanor was the first to speak. "You've bought a test?" Her hands were clutched together in front of her.

Gravely, Brooke nodded. "I have indeed."

Charlie's smile dropped. "You're not pregnant?"

Brooke still had the white stick in her hand and showed it to Charlie. The next minute, three shrieks sliced the air.

"What the hell?" A tousled-looking Blake walked in, Logan on his heels.

"What's going on?"

"Brooke's pregnant!" Charlie sang, and hugged her husband.

"It's one test," Brooke said. "I'll go and see the doctor when I'm home, but yeah, I think I'm pregnant."

Grinning, Logan stepped forward and hugged them both. "Happy for you. I'll open up another bottle of bubbly." Charlie followed him out of the room.

"Congratulations," Blake said. "Life on the ranch is going to be interesting one of these days."

"Oooh, I'm so happy for you!" Lindsay sang, kissing them both. "Come on, Blake, let's make breakfast."

Eleanor was crying openly, tears running down her face. "I'm so, so happy for the two of you." She first hugged Gavin and then Brooke.

Brooke's phone rang, and sniffling, she looked around for it. "Where's my phone?"

Grinning, Gavin picked up the ringing device, then frowned. "This isn't yours."

"I now have two phones!" She grinned, grabbing it from him. "It's Michelle. Sorry, I have to take this."

With another quick hug, Eleanor left the room.

Gavin sat down on the bed and inhaled deeply. Just a few hours before, he hadn't been sure what was going to happen. Last night, he'd had a plan. He was going to talk to Brooke, tell her how he felt about her and…

"Babe?" Brooke turned to look at him, taking her phone from her ear. There was a slight frown between her eyes. "Michelle says there is a very persistent client who wants the two paintings hanging behind the podium—you know the ones I'm talking about?"

Nodding, he got up and walked toward her. "Don't you want to sell them?"

"I thought no, but now…" She lifted the phone to her ear again. "Okay, Michelle, your client can have it."

While she finished the call, Gavin pulled her closer. He knew exactly where those two paintings would hang.

"I have to tell Connor about the baby," Brooke said.

"Let's tell him together?"

Just then the door opened, and Eleanor ushered Connor into the room. "He was asking for his mom."

Brooke patted the bed. "Come and sit, Connor. Gavin and I have something we want to tell you."

"Did I do something wrong?"

"No, sweetie, you haven't done anything wrong." Brooke smiled. "How would you feel about a baby brother or sister?"

Connor's eyes widened. "Does that mean I get another d—"

But Brooke quickly put a hand over his mouth. "It means you'll be an older brother."

"Breakfast's ready!" Charlie called.

Brooke got up, smiling. "I think I'm hungry. Coming?" She held out her hand to Gavin.

He pulled her close and they walked toward the kitchen, Connor running in front of them. So much was changing so fast, all in a positive direction...yet something wasn't quite right. He just couldn't put his finger on what.

CHAPTER 18

A week later, they were all back on the ranch, and life continued as usual. Well, everyone else was back, except for Gavin. He still had clients to see and was staying another week in Seattle. Since their arrival back on the ranch, Brooke was finding it difficult to settle down. She'd been to see the family doctor, and he'd confirmed she was indeed, pregnant.

She sat staring at the boxes in her bedroom she hadn't unpacked yet. She now knew what was missing in her house, in her room: Gavin's presence. Ever since she'd moved in, she'd unconsciously been looking for him everywhere. She wanted him to be here, with her and Connor and Baby.

Listlessly, she opened one of the boxes. Since she'd finished a painting that morning, she was at a loose end, not quite sure what to do next.

This one wasn't for any exhibition, but she was in love, not something she'd thought would ever be possible again. She had no choice but to try to express her intense emotions, and the only way she knew how was to put her feelings onto a canvas.

The painting would be a surprise for Gavin. It had

been a surprise for her, truth be told. When she'd picked up her palette knife Tuesday morning, she hadn't known what she was going to paint. Her only thought had been to get her feelings on to the canvas.

She should've felt more relaxed by now. But...what was going to happen next? Was something going to happen? She had no idea. Normally, she took things in her stride; she was never overly concerned about what tomorrow would bring. Things seemed to happen whether she fretted or not, she'd discovered a long time ago. But now she was agonizing over the uncertainty of "what now," and it was driving her crazy.

Gavin seemed very happy with Baby: he was attentive and loving, and she heard from him at least a few times a day, asking how she was. He missed her; he couldn't wait to see her again. But was this how things were going to work? She was pregnant with his baby, and he'd be cheering from the sides?

So far, she'd managed to stop Connor from asking whether Gavin was going to be his new dad, but she wasn't sure whether she'd be able to do that the next time.

She also had questions she didn't know the answers to, damn it.

They'd all had a lovely weekend in Seattle, but she and Gavin had never been alone during the day. There were people around them all the time and during the night; neither one of them had wanted to waste time talking.

He'd taken them to the airport. He'd told her they had to talk, but it had been five days, and she still had no idea what he wanted to talk about and when they'd be able to talk. When exactly he would be back on the ranch was another unanswered question.

At least she was feeling much better. The worst of the nausea seemed to have passed, and she could eat again.

There was a knock on her front door. "Anyone home?" Charlie called out.

Smiling, Brooke got up quickly and walked out of her

room. She loved the easy way they all got along, and either of her sisters-in-law dropping by always brightened her day.

Both Lindsay and Charlie were in the living room. "Hello." Lindsay smiled. "We haven't seen you around much this week."

"I've been painting, and now I'm trying to settle in, but I just want to sleep. Come on in, I'll make tea."

In the kitchen, Lindsay pulled out a chair. "So why aren't we organizing a wedding yet?"

Brooke shook her head. "I don't think there's going to be one."

Charlie opened the cupboard and took out cups and saucers. "But that's ridiculous—of course, there'll be a wedding."

Brooke concentrated on the ritual of making tea. She wanted to bawl her eyes out, but that wasn't going to change anything. "It is what it is. Gavin has been very clear right from the start about not getting married."

"But he loves you!" Lindsay cried.

"I know. And he's said he always wants to be with me, but that doesn't mean he's changed his mind about getting married. Look, I've done that. If Gavin doesn't want that, I'm okay. I suppose not every love story ends in a ring, a wedding, and flowers, you know?"

"And you're happy with that?"

"I'm happy." She grinned. "I'm pregnant, and I feel miserable most afternoons, but I'm really happy."

Charlie looked at Lindsay. "Who's she trying to convince?"

As Brooke poured the tea, a huge lump settled in her throat. These freaking hormones were making her leak tears all the time.

"So if you're so happy, why are you crying?" Charlie asked.

"I'm…" A soft sob escaped. "I'm not unhappy, it's just…" And to her chagrin, she burst into tears.

ELSA WINCKLER

"What have you said to her?" someone bellowed close by.

Gavin? But it couldn't be—he was still in Seattle. A pair of strong, comforting arms pulled her close, and another sob escaped. Outside, Bear, Sasha, and Lucy were barking like crazy.

"What happened?" he asked. "Did you say something to upset her?"

"She said you don't want to get married," Lindsay said.

"And according to her, not every love story ends with a ring and wedding," Charlie added.

"What the hell? Brooke, babe?" He lifted her face with his hands. "I haven't had a chance to talk to you, damn it, but of course, I want to marry you."

Sniffing, she looked up at him. "You do?"

"Why do you think I stayed behind for five days? I had to get the ring sized and cleaned and…" Cussing under his breath, he glared at his sisters. "You two have messed up my whole speech, damn it."

Charlie was chuckling, clearly enjoying the situation. "You haven't made a speech yet. Have I missed anything, Linds?"

"No, you haven't. I haven't seen the ring or heard him—"

"Mom! Is Gavin here? His truck is outside, and the dogs are going crazy." Connor burst through the front door at full speed. "Uncle Gavin—you're here!" Rushing forward, he hugged Gavin's legs.

With his heart not quite settled yet, Gavin crouched down in front of the little boy. He hated seeing Brooke unhappy, but damn it, he'd wanted this to be perfect. He'd already spoken to Logan and Brooke's mother, and he had a great plan: dinner at a restaurant, creating a romantic moment where he was going to ask Brooke to marry him, but now his two sisters had made her cry. He would have to forget about all his previous plans and do something quickly. It would seem there were still way too many misunderstandings between them.

He smiled at Connor. "I've missed you, too. I'm so glad you're here. You see, I have a question to ask you."

Connor nodded, gravely. "I have a question to ask you, too."

"Yeah? Well, ask away?"

"Will you be my new dad? You see, I don't have one anymore, and now that I'm getting a baby brother...or sister, we'll need a dad. You can cook, and you make Mom happy."

You could hear a pin drop. For once, his sisters were silent. Gavin had to swallow a few times before he was able to speak. He put a hand on Connor's small shoulder. "And I wanted to ask you if I could be your dad and marry your mom?"

"You'll be our baby's dad, too?"

Brooke moved closer and put a hand on his shoulder. Taking her hand in his, he nodded. "Of course."

"Okay, great! Mom, I'm hungry. Can...may Gavin cook for us?"

Everyone burst into laughter, and Gavin got up quickly. "Not quite yet. You see, I still have to ask your mom if she would marry me. And I'm not sure what she's going to say."

"Oh, okay. Ask her, I'm hungry."

Everyone laughed.

"I didn't think I'd have an audience"—he grinned at his sisters—"but it seems, in this family, nothing is sacred anyway." He took the small box out of his pocket before he touched Brooke's hand. With his gaze on her, he went down on one knee. "Brooke, I'm pretty sure I'm going to make mistakes and I'll mess up, a lot. But one thing I can promise you is that I'll spend my life loving you. I already love Connor, too, and even though I didn't think it was possible to love one more person, there is also a place in my heart for our unborn baby. I want to give you this ring, my mother's ring. If you want another one, as well, we can get you one, anytime. But please marry me?"

His sisters were yelling, the dogs were still barking hysterically outside, but Gavin kept his gaze steadily on Brooke. With a sob, she fell forward, and catching her in his arms, he stood them up, together.

He lifted her chin. "Is that a yes?"

"It's a yes." She smiled, tears streaming down her face. "Sorry, hormones. I never cry this much." She held out her hand, and he slid the ring home. A perfect fit. Grateful, he smiled at his two sisters.

Brooke promptly burst into tears again.

Frowning, he pulled her closer. "What's wrong? We can really get another ring…"

"I love my ring!" Brooke sobbed.

"Happy tears." Lindsay smiled.

Outside, the dogs were going mad.

"What's up with the dogs?" Charlie said, getting up. "Let me go and—"

But Gavin stopped her with his hand. "I know why they're barking." Looking down at Brooke, he wiped away her tears. "We haven't discussed this, but I hope you won't be mad."

Brooke frowned. "Mad about what?"

"Connor, come on. I have a surprise for you. Well, probably for your mom, as well." And with his arm around Brooke and Connor's hand in his, they walked outside, his sisters hot on their heels.

Bear and Sasha and Lucy were running around his SUV, barking hysterically. When they saw them coming out of the house, they went ballistic.

"Sasha! Bear! Lucy!" Charlie called, but the dogs ignored her.

Gavin quickly opened one of the doors in the back and took out a box. "Okay, guys, come and meet your new neighbor." He put the box on the ground and opened it.

The three dogs jumped up the sides of the box, yelping.

"A Labrador puppy!" Charlie rushed forward and picked up the small, wriggling puppy. "Oh, Connor, look." She bent down, picked up the puppy, and showed it to Connor.

Connor's eyes were like saucers when he looked at his mother. "Can I touch it?"

"You may." Brooke smiled.

Charlie put the puppy in the little boy's arms. "Can...may we keep it, Mom?"

Tears were again streaming down Brooke's cheeks as she nodded. Worried, Gavin pulled her close. "I should've asked you first..."

Smiling, she leaned against him. "Yes, you should've, but look at Connor's face. You're forgiven."

Kissing Brooke's temple, Gavin exhaled slowly as he watched Connor playing with the puppy. He'd heard about the puppies a while ago, and had asked the owner to keep one for him. At the time, he'd thought to get it for Connor, and if Brooke didn't want a puppy, he'd keep it himself. But now they were going to be a family, they were going to be together. Forever.

He waited for the panic to set in, but the only feeling he could identify was of overwhelming gratitude. With the puppy in his arms, Connor rushed toward his mom.

"Look, Mom. I have a puppy. Does it have a name, Uncle...Dad?"

Brooke caught her breath, and Gavin had to swallow a few times before he could speak. Crouching down in front of the little boy, he nodded. "I thought we could call him Jack...son, but it's your dog, you decide."

Connor smiled, petting the puppy. "Jack. I like it. Thanks, Dad."

Gavin picked up the boy and puppy and put an arm around Brooke. This beautiful, talented woman loved him; she was carrying his baby and had welcomed him to be a part of her small family, as well. He had a whole lifetime ahead of him to love them.

"So why are the dogs going crazy?" Eleanor asked behind them.

"I can't believe you've stayed away all this time." Charlie grinned and hugged her. "We have big news. Big. But..." She pointed toward Eleanor's face. "You probably know, don't you?"

"Granma, look, a puppy!" Connor cried out. "And Uncle Gavin is going to be my new dad and he's also going to be Baby's new dad. And we—"

Over Brooke's head, Gavin met his future mother-in-law's eyes. She was openly crying.

"Oh, I'm so happy to hear that," she sniffed, hugging them both. "When?"

"When what?" Gavin asked.

"When are you getting married?"

"As far as I'm concerned, tomorrow." Gavin smiled.

Brooke looked up at him. "Okay."

His smile slipped. "Okay?"

Brooke's eyes narrowed. "Are you backing out?"

He stared into her eyes for long moments, and there in the depths, he could see she really meant it. She was going to marry him. Tomorrow.

"Tomorrow it is." He kissed her.

Connor groaned. "Ew, I suppose that's going to happen all the time now?"

Gavin grinned against Brooke's mouth. "Oh, yes."

"You are crazy!" Lindsay laughed. "You can't marry tomorrow. Okay, I know that's exactly what—"

"—You and Blake did," Eleanor finished her sentence.

"What about a dress?" Charlie asked. "We could drive to Bozeman quickly, and—"

Eleanor lifted her hand, smiling. "I've actually bought you a dress."

"Mom!" Brooke gasped. "I remember you'd said you've seen a dress, but I didn't know you'd actually bought it. At the time, Gavin and I were still in a fake relationship!"

Eleanor hugged her. "Everyone else could see it was the real thing. You two just had to figure out the details. You'll love the dress, I promise."

Brooke laughed. "I'm sure I will. So now you're done interfering in everyone else's life, I think it's time we find you a husband."

"Yes!" Lindsay cried.

"Fabulous idea," said Charlie. "You have someone in mind, Brooke?"

"I do. And I'll make sure he's your date tomorrow, Mom."

Eleanor looked really worried. She put a hand on Brooke's arm. "Brooke, sweetheart, now don't be silly, I'm old and—"

Brooke interrupted her. "—Fabulous, and clearly not busy enough."

"I don't have any intention of interfering in anyone else's life, although I was wondering about Jared and Stacy."

"Who's Jared and Stacey?" Gavin asked.

"Jared is Blake's friend. He's also involved in the dojo, and Stacey is another ex-South African who has recently relocated to Alisson."

"They'll be perfect for each other." Eleanor's eyes twinkled.

Brooke rolled her eyes. "Mom, seriously." She grabbed her mom's hand. "Come on, we have a wedding to plan."

As they walked away, Brooke glanced over her shoulder at him and winked. His heart just about jumped out of his chest.

"Look at his silly grin," Lindsay teased.

Charlie smiled, her eyes bright with tears. "I wish Mom and Dad could see us now. All together again."

Lindsay put her arms around Gavin and Charlie. "I'm sure they can," she said, with a sniffle.

CHAPTER 19

It was another glorious summer's day. In the distance, the mountains rose high up into an azure blue sky with not a cloud in sight. Brooke jumped out of bed. She'd stayed with her mom the night before. Gavin had moved most of his things into her house yesterday. The rest, they'd pick up later.

Gavin had mentioned they could add a room or two to Brooke's house, seeing that there was no need to build one for him. But that was something to think about later; at the moment, she couldn't wait to marry her fiancé.

Charlie, Lindsay, and her mom had pampered her last night, and she now had soft hands, oil-paint-free nails and painted toenails. She lifted her hand and looked at the ring. On the top of a narrow golden band was a gorgeous ruby, surrounded by tiny diamonds. It was his mother's ring.

Gavin had invited the men for a barbeque, which he called a braai, at their house. Next time she walked into the house, Gavin would be there, as well.

Hugging herself, Brooke closed her eyes for a moment. Adam. He'd been a good man, a loving dad to Connor, and she'd always have a special place in her heart for him. She'd never thought she'd have a second chance at love, but then Charlie and Lindsay had moved to Alisson, and not long after, their brother had followed them. And even though she hadn't known it at the time, she'd fallen for this big, sexy South African the first time she'd seen him.

Some things were simply meant to be and had been written in the stars a long time ago.

Her bedroom door flew open, and her mother, Lindsay, and Charlie entered. All were still in their pajamas, and Charlie was carrying a tray with four coffee mugs.

"You're supposed to be still in bed!" laughed Lindsay. "We've brought coffee."

"Sounds amazing, thanks." She quickly got under the sheets again and took her mug from Charlie. "Mmm, I'm so glad I can drink coffee again."

"I remember the feeling." Charlie laughed. "I'm so glad you're feeling better. We can't have the bride sprinting for the bathroom every five minutes."

While everyone laughed, Lindsay handed her a small, square box. "From the bridegroom. He was here at the crack of dawn and very disappointed he couldn't see you."

"Why didn't you tell me? I'm sure it'll be okay," Brooke protested as she stared at the small box. "He doesn't have to give me another present; he's given me a ring. I didn't even expect that."

"Open it," Charlie urged her.

With unsteady fingers, Brooke opened the small package and lifted the lid of the small box. She lost her breath. "A chain with a ruby pendant. It's gorgeous."

Charlie leaned closer to look at it. "He says you seldom wear rings while you're painting, but this you can wear around your neck, and you'll always have something of his with you."

Brooke sniffed. "He's so thoughtful. Oh, my goodness, I'm crying again!"

Charlie jumped up. "Dry those tears. The makeup artist and hairdresser will be here any minute now, and then we can't cry again."

"Makeup artist and hairdresser?" Brooke asked.

Lindsay grinned. "Everyone in town will be right on their heels to help with the wedding. Your mother may be interfering, but nobody can say no to her."

"Thanks, Mom."

"I'm so happy for you."

Brooke winked at Charlie and Lindsay. "Make sure someone does Mom's hair and makeup, too, will you? Remember, she has a date."

"Brooke!" her mother cried. "Don't tell me…"

"Go on, make yourself pretty. I told you I'm getting you a date."

"Why would you do that? And who in his right mind would want to be my date? I can't believe you did that."

"Believe it." Charlie grinned. "We've learned from the best—you!"

"So who's my date?" her mother asked again.

"Who do you think?"

"I can't think of anyone…"

"A certain attorney who 'adores' you?"

"Guy?" her mom asked, her cheeks turning pink. "But that's ridiculous. I can't have a date. I'm way too old."

They all burst out laughing.

Brooke hugged her mom. "You'll never be old, trust me. Now go make yourself pretty."

Mumbling, her mother left the room, a giggling Charlie and Lindsay following her.

Brooke quickly put on the chain and pendant before she phoned her fiancé.

Bleary-eyed, Gavin looked at Connor and the puppy on the lawn outside. The little boy had been wide awake at six o'clock that morning and had woken Gavin up by putting the yelping puppy on his face.

He rubbed his neck. He probably had too much to drink last night, and he'd had way too little sleep, but he couldn't wait to see his bride. When he'd delivered her small gift earlier, he'd hoped to at least catch a glimpse of Brooke, but his sisters had quickly closed the door in his face, ignoring all his pleas.

The reason he wanted to see her was to reassure her of his feelings. There had been enough misunderstandings between them. He wanted her to be absolutely sure he loved her. Now he had to wait another few hours before he could tell her, damn it.

His phone rang. It was a video call from Brooke.

Excited, he answered. And nearly lost his last breath. He could only see her head and shoulders. His gift he'd dropped off earlier was around her neck, and it would seem that was all she was wearing. He caught his breath "Babe…what are you wearing?"

Her smile lit up his very soul. "Your present."

He swore softly. "And that's all?"

Her smile sent his blood roaring through his body. "Oh, yeah."

"You'll pay for this, you know that?"

"I can't wait."

"I love you."

Her eyes were bright with tears. "Love you, too. But now I have to go. I have to get ready for my bridegroom."

"We can always elope, you know?"

"Sorry—I want to get married to you today in front of the whole town. They've been gossiping about us long enough. We have to show them we're making this legal." She grinned. "See you later. I have a surprise for you tonight."

"So have I, babe, so have I."

He was still grinning like an idiot many minutes after they'd ended the call.

There was a huge marquee tent outside Logan and Charlie's house.

Brooke stopped as she and Logan walked out of his and Charlie's house. "Where did that come from?"

Logan grinned. "As with Blake and Lindsay's wedding, the whole town pitched in. Mom was on the phone for most of the night. I don't think she or Charlie or Lindsay have slept."

"I thought it would only be the family…"

"You know Mom. Happy?" he asked her.

"Very happy."

"Dad…" Logan inhaled deeply. "He would've been so proud of the woman you've become."

Brooke couldn't speak; her heart was overflowing. She put her head against her brother's shoulder.

"Ready?" he asked.

Swallowing the lump in her throat, she nodded. "So ready."

The three dogs, all sporting colored ribbons around their necks, were standing at the entrance of the tent. "Look at them, so cute. Where's Jack?"

Before Logan could answer, Connor appeared in the opening of the tent with Jack in his arms.

"She's here!" he yelled, and with the laughter of everyone in Alisson in the background, Brooke walked into the tent toward her bridegroom, her lover, her future.

It was late when Gavin carried her into their house. "You happy?" Slowly, he slid her down his body.

"Very happy. We had a beautiful wedding. And the whole town pitched in to help again. I didn't think we could do this a second time, but it was a great success."

"Have I told you how much I love your dress?" His gaze was on his fingers, tracing the upper line of her breasts just visible above the sweetheart neckline of the top.

Turning her slowly around, he played with the tiny buttons at the back of the dress. "These have been driving me crazy all night," he whispered. As his lips followed the line of her satiny shoulders, she sighed contentedly.

"You make me feel like the most beautiful woman on earth."

"That's because you are," he whispered, his fingers busy with the tiny buttons. "I love my sisters and I love your family, but I'm very glad to be alone with you, at last. And tomorrow, I'm taking you away for a few days."

She looked at him over her shoulder. "I didn't think you'd have time…"

"Logan, Charlie, and Ellie are going to Seattle for the next month. I have a few appointments with clients, but I can talk to them from anywhere. And your mom offered to look after Connor. All you have to do is pack your bikini."

"Where are you taking me?"

He chuckled as he steered her toward the living room. "That's a surprise. One of a few I have in store for you. The first one is right here," he said, switching on the living room lights.

Stunned, she couldn't speak for a few minutes. Her two paintings, *The Kiss* and *The Forever-Kind* were hanging on one of the walls of the living room.

She turned to Gavin. "You were the persistent customer?"

"I am. I'm no art critic, babe, but I couldn't let anyone else have these two—this is us, isn't it?"

She nodded.

He pulled her closer. "I love us. I love your paintings, and I love, I love you."

"I love you, too. Time for my surprise." As she took his hand, she could feel her dress slipping. Her bridegroom had been busy; he'd unbuttoned her dress all the way down, it would seem. She held it up with one hand as she led him down the corridor to her studio.

"Turn around," she ordered him. "I'll tell you when you can look."

Grinning, he obeyed.

Yesterday, when she'd finished the painting, she'd put it against the wall, the front turned away from prying eyes. She'd wanted to keep it a surprise for Gavin. Lifting the painting while managing to keep her dress from slipping down wasn't that easy, but finally the painting was on the easel.

"Okay, you can look now."

Slowly, he turned around. His eyes widened. "Babe..." He walked closer, staring at the painting.

She'd painted him as she saw him—caring, gentle, loving, compassionate. All these attributes were in his eyes, in the way he smiled from the painting.

"Is that really how you see me?" His voice wasn't quite steady.

She stepped forward. "Loving, caring, always there when I need you? Yes, that's exactly how I see you. That's exactly who you are. You're a great catch, Gavin Wilson, and I'm so glad you agreed to have a fake relationship with me weeks ago." And she dropped the dress.

His eyes darkened. Stepping over the dress, he picked her up. "Thank you, babe. I will do my utmost to live up to this picture."

She slid her hands behind his neck. "Starting now, I hope?"

"Starting right now." And kissing her, he strode purposefully toward their bedroom.

"Have I told you that you make my toes curl when you kiss me?" she asked against his lips.

Laughing, he put her down next to the bed. "You'll have to show me."

"You'll have to take my shoes off."

"Gladly, Mrs. Wilson, gladly. I will spend my life loving you and making sure your toes are always, always curling."

"Deal," she whispered, and kissed him.

ACKNOWLEDGEMENTS

Thanks again to Melissa Keir and Inkspell Publishing, I'm so happy I've found you.

I also want to thank you, dear reader, for your continued support and lovely feedback – without you writing stories wouldn't have been early as much fun.

And as always, thanks to my own real-life hero, Theo who still reads every word – you make it so easy to write about love.

DON'T MISS THE OTHER BOOKS IN THE UNEXPECTED LOVE SERIES

KISSING CHARLIE: #1

One Kiss Will Change Their Lives Forever

Bowen therapist Charlie Wilson is not interested in men or relationships. Her only concern is making sure her sister Lindsay is safe.

But then billionaire Logan Johnson walks into her rooms and stirs powerful feelings inside of her. Logan's perfectly knotted tie is a clear indication free-spirit Charlie should steer clear of him at all costs.

They are complete opposites, so why does he keep coming back to see her?

EXCERPT:

"How did you hurt your back?" Her voice was cool, and she wasn't meeting his eyes.

"While hiking," he said curtly. He was in pain; it didn't matter what the hell happened. "Tell me about this

Wowen, Bowen, whatever the hell you call this cr—therapy."

She gave him a cool look. "It's called Bowen Therapy."

"Bowen Therapy," he said, his gaze on her mouth.

"The guiding principles of the technique were established by Tom Bowen during the 1950s. It focuses on the whole person, not just the condition. In other words, it treats the cause, not only the symptoms. It helps the body to heal and restores the balance by shifting the body from your innate 'fight or flight' system to a more natural state of calm."

He watched her as she studied his body. She was holding something in her hand. Damn, she had yet to touch him, but he was struggling not to react to her nearness. The fact that he was lying on his back wasn't helping, either.

"Natural state of calm? With you doing strange things to my body?" he grumbled, only realizing the ambiguity of his words when they hung in the air around them.

Her lips twitched.

"Oh, you think this is funny?" he snarled.

"I think you're in pain. I think you like being in control and at the moment, you're not. That's why you feel the need to lash out. But it's fine. I often have children throwing tantrums."

"I'm not throwing a tantrum, damn it…" He tried to sit up straight, but a pain shot up his back, and groaning, he had to slowly lie down again.

"The movements in Bowen Therapy," she continued as if he hadn't interrupted her, "are very distinctive and are used on precise points on the body. It involves moving the soft tissue in a particular way. I will use a rolling-type movement, using my fingers, hands, or sometimes my elbow. It will create a focus for the brain by stimulating the nerve pathways and tissue. I work on only a small area, depending how far your skin can move. What you may find strange—"

"This whole damn day is strange. I don't know what the hell my mother was thinking," he muttered.

PROTECTING LINDSAY: #2

How does he protect his heart while protecting her?

Lindsay Wilson simply wants to concentrate on her shop where she sells her own mixtures of creams and essential oils. What she doesn't want is the seriously sexy Blake Davidson hell-bent on protecting her from the abusive boyfriend who followed her to Montana all the way from South Africa. To add to her frustration, he makes her feel things she's never felt before but she's made a mistake in the past, can she trust her instincts this time?

Blake lost two people before because he couldn't protect them, so what's different this time with Lindsay? From the moment he's laid eyes on her, all his instincts have been telling him to make sure nothing happens to her so he has no choice but to move into her place and keep her safe. But what about his own heart?

EXCERPT:

For the first time, she really looked at him. Oh, my. He'd grown a beard since she'd last seen him. She'd never liked beards, but on this tall, dark, and ridiculously attractive guy, it only added to his smoldering good looks.

Grinding her teeth to make sure her jaw wouldn't drop, she turned away. "So, which essential oils are you interested in buying today?"

Here she was, a grown woman, just about salivating because a gorgeous man was in her shop. Maybe she should seriously begin to think about dating again. "There is an essential oil for just about every problem you may have. Suzie's husband, for instance…" The minute the words left her mouth, Lindsay nearly groaned out loud. Normally, she kept clients' issues completely confidential, but Suzie had already let that cat way out of the bag. Even so, why talk about Suzie's bedroom problem, of all things, while she was talking to Blake?

"I don't have problems in the bedroom." His voice was as smooth as Tennessee whiskey.

Lindsay closed her eyes for a minute. He didn't have to tell her that; one look at his broad shoulders, square jaw, and confident stride made it clear he was all man and… Oh, my goodness, the very last thing she should be thinking about was Blake and bedrooms.

"Okay, so maybe something for your beard?" Why didn't she simply shut up? She motioned to one of the shelves. "I make a very nice oil with lavender, peppermint, lemon, and coconut oil. You should try it."

"I don't…" he began gruffly, before he swore softly and took out his wallet. "Okay, give me the damn oil."

Available Where Books Are Sold…

ABOUT THE AUTHOR

Elsa has been reading love stories for as long as she can remember and when she 'met' the classic authors like Jane Austen, Elizabeth Gaskell, Henry James, The Brontë sisters, etc. during her English Honours studies, she was hooked for life.

She married her college boyfriend and soul mate and after 46 years, 3 interesting and wonderful children and 4 beautiful grandchildren, they are now fortunate to live in the picturesque little seaside village of Betty's Bay, South Africa.

She likes the heroines in her stories to be beautiful, feisty, independent and headstrong. And the heroes must be strong but possess a generous amount of sensitivity. They are of course, also gorgeous! Her stories typically incorporate the family background of the characters to better understand where they come from and who they are when we meet them in the story.

Webpage: www.elsawinckler.com
Personal Facebook page:
https://www.facebook.com/elsa.winckler
Author Facebook page:
https://www.facebook.com/ElsaWincklerRomanceAutho
r?ref_type=bookmark
Twitter: https://twitter.com/elsawinckler @elsawinckler
Goodreads:
https://www.goodreads.com/author/show/6557709.Elsa
_Winckler
Pinterest: http://www.pinterest.com/elsawinckler/
Wattpad: http://www.wattpad.com/user/elsaw1
Instagram: https://www.instagram.com/elsaw1/